Lily B.
on the
Brink of
Paris

Also by Elizabeth Cody Kimmel

Lily B. on the Brink of Cool
Lily B. on the Brink of Love

ELIZABETH CODY KIMMEL

Lily B.
on the
Brink of
Paris

HarperCollins Publishers

The lines on page 134 are from Jim Morrison's "The End," as recorded by The Doors.

Lily B. on the Brink of Paris
Copyright © 2006 by Elizabeth Cody Kimmel
For information address
HarperCollins Children's Books, a division of HarperCollins
Publishers, 1350 Avenue of the Americas, New York, NY 10019.
www.harpercollinschildrens.com

Library of Congress Cataloging-in-Publication Data
Kimmel, Elizabeth Cody.
    Lily B. on the brink of Paris / Elizabeth Cody Kimmel.—1st ed.
        p.   cm.
    Summary: On a class trip to France, fourteen-year-old Lily is
determined to gather material for her great Parisian novel, but her
daydreaming and lack of attention get her into trouble when she
becomes separated from her group.
    ISBN-10: 0-06-083948-1 (trade bdg.)
    ISBN-13: 978-0-06-083948-2 (trade bdg.)
    ISBN-10: 0-06-083949-X (lib. bdg.)
    ISBN-13: 978-0-06-083949-9 (lib. bdg.)
    [1. School field trips—Fiction.   2. Paris (France)—Fiction.]
I. Title.
PZ7.K56475Lp 2006   2005037026
[Fic]—dc22   CIP
                                                          AC

Typography by Amy Ryan
1 2 3 4 5 6 7 8 9 10

First Edition

To Patricia Donohue

Lily B.
on the
Brink of
Paris

One

Everything I know about Paris, I've learned from my Madeline books. I know, for example, that it is not unusual for houses in Paris to be covered with vines. I know that if you are a parentless little girl, you can go to stay with Miss Clavel, the nun, and walk around the city with your yellow-hatted homegirls in two perfectly straight lines. I know that if you develop appendicitis in the dead of night, caring medical assistance is rapidly available.

But the most notable thing about the Madeline books is that Paris served as the author's inspiration. And if Paris can do that for Ludwig Bemelmans, it can do it for me, too. Yes, Dear Readers, my Great Parisian Novel will soon be born, because the time has come for Lily Blennerhassett to get serious about writing. The world cannot be expected to wait much longer. I have honed my craft by keeping diaries and penning advice columns, but the subjects I wrote about weren't really Life Experiences of International Interest. A trip to Paris, however, is a whole other story. Things of International Interest HAPPEN in Paris. After all, it is the City of Lights. The model for all that is elegant and timeless. The archetype for true culture and sophistication, the kind that we in America lost somewhere between the Big Mac and the Starbucks Frappuccino.

I don't have a plot yet. But I'm not going to worry about that. My job is to search out gems and nuggets of Paris at its most elegant and mysterious. Then I will add them to my Mental Pool. There are heated pools, public pools, aboveground pools, and wading pools, but to my knowledge I am the only individual in my school district with a Mental Pool. This is where I collect all my gems and nuggets and store them for later literary use. My Mental Pool already contains many amusing and baffling gems and nuggets. But I don't think any of them are novelworthy. Mark my words, my Parisian Mental Pool gems and nuggets *will* be novelworthy. And I will find Extraordinary Characters. Because our little group making up the Mulgrew Middle School Paris Class Trip is not exactly brimming with Extraordinary Characters.

There were eight of us—nine if you counted the

chaperone—enjoying the luxurious accommodations provided by John F. Kennedy International Airport's Terminal 1. Let me describe them to you, Dear Reader:

Traveler Number One. First, and most important, me. Lily Blennerhassett. I am, naturally, the Official Diarist of the trip. The Immortalizer of our Exploits. The Recorder of our Recreation. The Accountant of our Antics. Nothing will escape my keen eye or my razor wit. Years hence readers wanting more after devouring my Great Parisian Novel will peruse my original diary entries, and Paris will spring to life before them. The pages themselves will smell lightly of Dijon mustard and baguettes. Ernest Hemingway said that "Paris is a movable feast." In the hands of the capable yet hip Lily Blennerhassett, I predict the city will be upgraded to a Snack Bar on Wheels. So we've got that going for us. And that's good.

Traveler Number Two. Charlotte McGrath. Locator of Passports, Instant Calculator of euro to dollar value, and Vault of Information regarding the cultural and legal guidelines within which we will find ourselves in France. Also my best friend. Shrink, parole officer, and life coach in one. A must on any transatlantic journey.

Traveler Number Three. Bonnie Roberts. Astral Traveler, Channeler of Universal Messages, and New Age Wise Woman. Has the tannest feet of any human being not currently famous I've ever seen. Brings new level of chic to peasant blouses and ankle bracelets. And, notably, sister of Jake. Through the injustice of our society's fixation on birth dates, Jake is literally in a different class from me. He's fifteen, a year older. And therefore not qualifiable to join the eighth (soon to be ninth) grade class trip. He had his own class trip last year actually, to Italy. Please ponder the Magnificent Wrongness of this: I travel to the city known throughout the world for its Celebration of Romance, and for the first time in my life I HAVE a boyfriend. But he must remain at home. Oh, how it plagues me! I cannot continue this paragraph.

Traveler Number Four. Janet Graham. Obsessed with All That Is French. Professional Irritant of the First Degree. Teacher's Pet. Also, insists on her name being pronounced Jah-nay Gra-hahmme. Utterly ridiculous.

Traveler Number Five: Lewis Pilsky. Computer God. Poster Child for the Internet Generation. Walking Pillar of Geekdom. Not the cutest boy on the block, but he means well. Small for his age, but try to pretend you don't notice.

Travelers Number Six and Seven: Bud and Chaz, the Football Guys. Attending this school trip because it may prevent them from failing Intro to French. Become animated only when discussing professional sports. Heads suspiciously jar shaped.

Traveler Number Eight: We call him the Mysterious Tim. Last name unknown. Has attended Mulgrew for only one year. To the knowledge of everyone I've asked, Tim has never spoken to anybody, though once a rumor circulated that the friend of a girl whose brother used to be in my literature class heard him say thank you to the lunch lady when she gave him extra Tater Tots. Whatever. Can't take gossip too seriously.

So you see, our little Paris group will not be flocking together, as we are not exactly birds of a feather. I'm not sure we're even members of the same species. But variety is the spice of life, or so they tell me. Did I mention my name? It's Lily Blennerhassett, Writer Extraordinaire.

After what seemed to be an unnecessarily prolonged period of agonizing at the gate, we were advised via loud-speaker to board the plane. I know it may come as a kind of shock, Dear Readers, since I have such a worldly air about me, but I had never actually been on an airplane before. The Blennerhassetts live a simple life. It is an unspoken rule in our household that any viable destination of the Blennerhassett clan must be reachable by our two-door Honda hatchback. If a body of water or a mountain range lies in the way, we just don't go there. But the Blennerhassetts as parents are also zealous believers in the Educational Experience, as shown by our family's Frequent Outings to yarn-making seminars and walking tours sponsored by local historical societies. So they were rather quick to agree that the Mulgrew Middle School Paris Class Trip was the ultimate Educational Experience. That is how I found myself sitting on a 747 between a future corporate executive and a flower child.

"I hope they remembered to get gas," remarked Bonnie.

Apparently Bonnie had never flown before either. I think transatlantic flight really did seem this simple to her, just a road trip with modified equipment. She probably imagined the pilot standing out in front of the plane with the hood up, checking the engine and unfolding a map of Europe with "Paris" circled in red Magic Marker while sipping on a 7-Eleven Big Gulp.

"Girls, seat belts," ordered Charlotte, as she counted and re-counted the number of rows between our seats and the closest emergency exit.

As we complied, little video monitors emerged from the ceiling overhead, screens flickering.

"Oooh, television," I said. Nobody had told me airplanes had TV. I find it impossible not to stare at a television that is on, and I'm not ashamed to admit it. A Writer must keep apprised of popular culture. A Writer must have her finger on the pulse of the masses. A Writer must watch MTV, the barometer of American youth. I needed to know what trend trolls like Lindy Sloane (Singer/Actress/Celebrity Personality) were listening to, what clubs they were getting tossed out of, what color their hair had turned "for a role," how scary skinny they'd become while claiming to eat everything—all the time—and never work out. I sat back and waited for Lindy Sloane's orange, bony, formerly freckled face to appear on-screen. My seatmates took no notice. Charlotte was intensely studying the laminated safety card she had found in the seat back. Bonnie appeared to be making some sort of origami bird out of her barf bag.

Sadly, they didn't seem to be showing anything interesting on the television. Certainly nothing about Lindy Sloane. In fact it wasn't MTV at all. As far as I could gather, it was an airline safety program about a little family of blond travelers, experiencing what appeared to be moderate to serious plane malfunction with unfailing good cheer. The family members were shown fastening seat belts with twinkles in their eyes, retrieving their oxygen masks and placing them over their noses and mouths merrily, and removing flotation devices from beneath their seats with toothy, affectionate smiles. From what I could see, there was apparently little more entertaining to this family than sudden cabin depressurization.

I don't know about you, Dear Readers, but I don't particularly like being REMINDED of what might go wrong in an airplane when my flight is about to take off. I don't want to come within ten feet of an oxygen mask or a flotation device. As for the logic of wearing a seat belt in case we take a sudden plunge from thirty thousand feet, well, I'm simply baffled. That's sort of like shutting the barn door after the horse has gotten out, don't you think?

Lindy Sloane travels by private jet.

"Let me see your seat belt," said Charlotte. "If you leave too much slack, it defeats the purpose."

I endured Charlotte's examination patiently. I knew from experience not to share my lack of faith in safety protocol with her. Charlotte is strictly a By the Book girl. Whereas me, I'm more of a Buy the Book girl.

Charlotte tugged on my belt.

"Tighter," she commanded. I made a little motion that simulated adjusting my seat belt.

"Tighter," she repeated. I did it again.

She was onto my pantomime. She reached for the long end of my seat belt herself and tugged it vigorously, cinching it in. I felt like I'd just been strapped into a Victorian corset and had spontaneously dropped two dress sizes.

"Charlotte! That's my bladder!" I shouted.

"Safety first," she replied, already back to studying her safety card.

Obviously, any further interaction with Charlotte was dangerous to my health, so I turned to Bonnie. Her eyes were closed, but her lips seemed to be moving.

"Bonnie?"

She opened one pale-blue eye and took me in.

"What are you doing?" I asked.

"Establishing a heart link with Michael."

Had Bonnie met a Boy?

"Who's Michael?" I inquired eagerly.

Bonnie opened her other eye.

"Michael is the governing archangel of safety and protection," she replied, as matter-of-factly as if she were discussing her shoe size. "I'm requesting a blessing for our flight."

The archangel of safety and protection? Did we need safety and protection? Were we going to experience moderate to serious plane malfunction like the blond people in the video?

Bonnie examined my expression. "If you're prone to anxiety attacks, Michael is a good angel to call on," she said.

Good grief.

"Just, uh, put in a good word for me," I said.

Bonnie nodded serenely and closed her eyes. Her lips started moving again.

I began to contemplate the drawbacks of continuing this seating arrangement for the duration of the seven-hour flight. I looked around the plane. It seemed fairly full. As I was considering the viability of spending the flight in the bathroom, a wide, sinister shape suddenly loomed over me. I let out a little shriek.

"*Eh bien*? Why ze scream?"

"Madame Chavotte!"

Madame Chavotte, our French teacher and our trip chaperone. Doesn't the name Chavotte bring to mind a delicate, prancing creature bathed in light? Well, forget it. Madame Chavotte was built like a tank, artillery included. She was as tall as a man and half again as wide. She usually wore a severe expression, which was enhanced by the single graying eyebrow that did not bother to pause over the bridge of her nose. Her hair, steel-wool gray, was pulled back in a bun so tight, it looked like she'd had a face-lift.

Had she asked me a question? The memory of it had been scared out of me. Madame Chavotte was almost always displeased with me. My mouth hung partially open, and I surrendered to the stupor.

"And why do you 'ave ze mouth 'anging open like ze Frankenstein?" she demanded.

I closed it. Overhead came the announcement that we were preparing for takeoff. Madame Chavotte shook her head like she disagreed with that assessment and pointed a thick, powerful finger at each of us.

"*Quatre, cinq, six,*" she counted. Then she moved away,

like a rhinoceros suddenly breaking off an attack, down the aisle to continue her head count. I breathed a sigh of relief. Jake was SO right to take Italian instead of French. His teacher, Signor Lucci, was as mild mannered as Mister Rogers. But swarthier.

Over the seat back in front of me, a face appeared like the Loch Ness Monster surfacing from the deep to menace and terrify the innocent.

"*Bonjour! Comment ça va?*"

I gave Janet my most convincing scowl. It wasn't too difficult, given that with Charlotte's modification my seat belt was compressing my bladder in a most agonizing fashion.

"We're about to take off!" Janet gushed. "Isn't it *vraiment fantastique?*"

"If you say so, Janet."

"It's Jah-nay," she said, smiling patiently. "I've got this book you just HAVE to read."

"I've brought plenty of my own—"

But it was too late. Janet was rummaging around in her bag. She produced a hardcover book and waved it triumphantly in the air.

"We've all got to read this. *C'est formidable.* You're the fastest reader, Lily, so you take it first."

I peeked at the title and recoiled.

"You want me to read a book called *French Women*

Don't Get Fat?" I exclaimed. "What are you trying to say, Janet?"

"It's Jah-nay," she corrected. "We will learn to nibble at our cheese, to savor tiny portions of *le chocolat*, to slowly sip a glass of fine wine. This is how we keep ourselves trim and chic in Paris."

Clearly Madame Chavotte had not read this book.

"We're not old enough to drink wine," I said. Janet ignored my comment.

"We are visiting the home of the legendary representative of French culture, Edith Piaf! We must be worthy of the greatest singer in French history! We must learn to live *comme les Françaises!*" she shouted.

The sound caused Charlotte to drop her safety card abruptly.

"Janet!" she said sternly. "Weren't you listening to the announcement? Fasten your seat belt and return your seat to the upright position. Immediately!"

Unable to produce a suitable French phrase in response to this command, Janet disappeared, and I heard her seat belt clicking into place.

"It's Jah-nay," I said wickedly.

Charlotte rolled her eyes, making me remember why I loved her.

The plane gave a little lurch and began to move in earnest. I was suddenly overwhelmed with anxiety and an unexpected pang of homesickness. I thought of my parents, the neurotic but lovable Phyllis and Lenny Blennerhassett. They had taken me to the airport, my father concentrating on driving precisely at the speed limit while my mother issued a stream of instructions, including but not limited to: Stay with the group; make your bed every morning; don't spend all your pocket money on the first day; take pictures; stay with the group; dress neatly; don't eat any raw fish; avoid Parisian boys; and again, for good measure, stay with the group. I thought of Milo, my beloved beagle, who had tenderly licked my suitcase from top to bottom before I left. I thought of Jake, who was away on a rock-climbing trip that prevented the poignant, misty-eyed farewell scene I'd imagined. What if he met some Rock-climbing Girl while I was away? Someone lithe and muscular who was not afraid of heights? I clutched my stomach with both hands at the thought.

The plane began to taxi down the runway. I had a brief, vivid image of my mother jogging behind the plane, waving frenetically and shouting, "Remember to stay with the group!" I forgot about Jake meeting a Rock-climbing Girl and began to giggle uncontrollably. Bonnie looked at me with tranquil concern.

"Anxiety attack?" she asked.

"Early-onset insanity," I replied, and Bonnie nodded as if she'd known all along.

Our plane, poised on the runway, began the sudden acceleration to takeoff. My mind filled with a cycling montage of images: brief trailers from every disaster movie I'd ever seen; grim-faced newscasters reporting an aviation tragedy; a physics professor explaining the scientific impossibility of 380 tons of steel's lifting into the air. The plane appeared to be vibrating like a food processor. The noise got really loud. I gripped my armrests as we went faster. I, Lily Blennerhassett, was freaking out.

To my right Charlotte was flipping through a copy of *Business Week*, looking as relaxed as a cruise ship passenger taking a little sun on the lido deck. To my left Bonnie was shuffling a deck of tarot cards, her expression Buddha-like. My two closest friends were not afraid to fly. Between the two of them they had knowledge spanning from the Federal Aviation Safety Guidelines to the Effects of Karma on Personal Well-being. If they weren't worried, I shouldn't be either.

So I closed my eyes and did a little work on my acceptance speech for the Pulitzer Prize in Fiction I'll win in ten or twenty years for my Great Parisian Novel. I had brought tears to my own eyes with my humble poignance when I felt a light, fluffy sensation in my stomach. The plane had stopped vibrating. Something had smoothed out.

"We're in the air," Charlotte said, without looking up from her magazine.

Lily B., on the Brink of Paris.

FROM THE PARISIAN DIARY OF
Lily M. Blennerhassett

We are on our way! In only seven hours we will arrive in Paris. Our flight has just lifted off, borne skyward by magnificent wings that give one thought of the condor, that regal and powerful bird. Yes, Paris awaits us, but until then I will relax in my seat and dream of croissants and the river Seine and all the lovely delights that await us.

I love flying. I could not be happier.

Just as I was closing my journal, the plane lurched, and I uttered a long, high-pitched scream. Janet's face popped up in front of me.

"It's only *la turbulence*!"

"*La* shut up!" I cried with dignity.

On the Brink of Paris indeed.

Two

There is nothing quite so damaging to one's personal dignity as being awakened by a flight attendant announcing the final approach to Paris, only to discover that a salad plate–size drool stain has appeared on one's shirt. I spent the time wading through Customs and Passport Control trying to hide my saliva display with my right hand. I must have looked like I was continuously reciting the Pledge of Allegiance to myself.

By the time we reached baggage collection, the stain had faded slightly but gone darker around the edges. It now looked like a topographical map of the island of Madagascar.

"Alors, mes enfants," Madame Chavotte was barking, "you are each responsible for your own bag, *oui?"*

The conveyor belt had begun to run, and a series of suit-cases magically appeared, one at a time, moving briskly along like little soldiers. I noticed with dismay that almost every suitcase was an identical discreet black. Just like mine. Except for one, which was a brilliant rainbow of tie-dyed colors.

"There's mine, man," Bonnie said, retrieving the neon psychedelic valise.

Bud and Chaz, the Football Guys, had also gotten their luggage, massive duffel bags with "New York Yankees" emblazoned on the side.

"Pay attention," Charlotte told me, watching the lug-gage belt like a hawk. I was beginning to despair of ever identifying my bag, until I saw one coming toward me wrapped in a giant neon-pink ribbon with "LILY BLENNERHASSETT" inked onto it. Phyllis Blenner-hassett had left her mark.

I grabbed the bag and turned to find the Mysterious Tim standing silently a few feet away. He was wearing a dark T-shirt and dark pants, and he was standing with his hands clasped in front of him. He looked like a mortician waiting for the funeral to start.

"Allons-y, allons-y!" Madame Chavotte was calling. This was a woman who had no need for a bullhorn. Hikers in Switzerland could probably hear her. She was gesturing energetically with both arms in the direction we were

supposed to *allons-y*. If I hadn't known better, I'd have thought she was performing some kind of mystical, aboriginal fertility dance.

Bonnie linked her arm through mine and gave me a dreamy smile.

"It's all starting, man," she said. "Our adventure of the spirit. I think I had a past life in Paris. Hey, look! Charlotte's the Man!"

Charlotte had earned the respected designation of "the Man" by appropriating a baggage cart, which she was wheeling toward us in a frenzy of organizational competence.

"Let's go, people!" she commanded in a friendly way. "We don't want to get left behind."

Phyllis Blennerhasset forfend we should become Separated from the Group.

Janet descended upon us with a squeal.

"Oooo, can I put my bag on the cart too? Can you believe we're really in Paree? Are you jet-lagged? Did you finish reading the book, Lily? My goodness, Bonnie, are those Birkenstocks on your feet? We've got to get you into some proper French *chaussures*."

Charlotte prevented any further stream of Janet's partially Frenchified verbal spew by deftly grabbing her bag, tossing it on top of our cart, and marching purposefully toward the exit, where Madame Chavotte was still wildly

 18

gesturing. Bonnie and I followed Charlotte out the door. I noticed Lewis was already standing in line at a bus stop. He was absorbed with his tiny portable computer, called a Sidekick. Lewis was rarely separated from the Internet.

"What's the haps, Lew?" I asked.

Lewis looked up, startled, like a kitten had just asked him for some spare change.

I pointed helpfully at the Sidekick, which was showing current news headlines.

"What's the news? What's going down?"

Lewis watched me for a moment, as if he wanted to make sure I wasn't making fun of him.

"They've discovered a new species of rodent in Laos," he said finally.

"Excellent!" I proclaimed, trying to make it sound like I'd been praying for this very event for months. I opened my mouth to contribute my opinion on such a tremendous triumph of naturalism, but Lewis had already bent his head over the Sidekick again, fingers tapping away on the itty bitty keyboard.

Bonnie and Charlotte were standing a few feet away, pulling bags off the luggage cart. Janet was standing there too, apparently speaking as her lips were moving and her eyebrows were zooming up and down. No one seemed to be listening to her, but Janet didn't appear to notice.

I heard the now-familiar sound of counting to the

number eight in French, issued in Madame Chavotte's thundering voice, making certain we were all present and accounted for.

When you're someplace foreign, it's nice to have someone in charge who knows things like what bus you're supposed to get on, even if that person is built like a linebacker and has only one eyebrow. A bus had stopped, and Madame Chavotte was interrogating the driver in lightning-speed French. Moments later the driver came down to the sidewalk, opened a compartment, and began to toss our bags inside.

"Allons!" cried Madame Chavotte. "Zis is our bus. Everyone get on it, pliz."

Interesting. Madame Chavotte didn't say "pliz" too often in America. Or "sank you," for that matter.

Bonnie, Charlotte, and I filed onto the bus together. We headed straight for the back row. Up front, I could see, the Mysterious Tim had slipped into a row by himself. When Bud and Chaz chose their seats, they both had to stoop to avoid smacking their jar-shaped heads on the luggage rack. Janet began to bounce toward our row enthusiastically but devised another plan at the last minute and plopped herself next to Madame Chavotte. I didn't see Lewis, but I could hear the telltale tap-tap-tapping that divulged his Internetaholic presence. Within minutes we were on something resembling a highway, which Janet shouted back to us was *la grand-route*.

We reached Paris in about forty minutes. I am ashamed to say I dozed off for most of the ride and awoke to find my Madagascar-shaped drool stain now more closely resembling the continent of Greenland. Charlotte was examining the information pack we'd each been mailed when we signed up for the trip. Milo, the beagle, had eaten most of mine, and I had no recollection of what I'd done with the rest of it. I wouldn't have read it anyway. Information packs were for Simple Tourists. Dear Readers, I want to state for the record that I, Lily Blennerhassett, am not now (nor ever will be) a Simple Tourist. I will not be among those of my peers who will purchase an Eiffel Tower snow globe or a beret with "I Love Paris" embroidered on the top. I will not be spending my euros acquiring shirts that say, "My friend went to Paris and all she got me was this lousy T-shirt." No Notre Dame key chains will make their way into my possession. You see, unlike my classmates, who have the luxury of being Simple Tourists, I am a Writer. A Writer who has frittered away the fourteen years since my birth producing Nothing of Lasting Literary Value. A Writer on the Brink of penning her First Masterpiece.

Charlotte would tell me everything I needed to know about the information pack, and I could keep my mind free for finding gems and nuggets for my Mental Pool. I leaned over her shoulder to refresh my memory on the facts of our stay. We were staying someplace called the Ville Ecole Internationale in the Parisian district called Le Marais. The bus was lumbering down a narrow street, and all around me were elegant beige buildings. With their grand arches and columns, they reminded me of wedding cakes. Old, sophisticated, beige wedding cakes. Occasionally a tan or yellow one. It was like . . . it was like . . .

"PARIS!" shouted Janet gleefully from the front of the bus. She must be as jet-lagged as the rest of us, forgetting to pronounce the name of the city like she usually did, in the French way, Paree.

Meanwhile, the bus had stopped. Which meant:

a. We were out of gas.
b. We had been stopped by *les bandits* intent on robbing each of us of our most valued possessions.
c. The bus driver had been beamed out of his seat and onto a spaceship that had been hovering, unnoticed, above our bus since we left the airport.
d. We had arrived at the Ville Ecole Internationale.

Turned out to be "d."

The VEI was sandwiched between two palatial-looking structures fit for royalty. The VEI itself, however, looked suspiciously like a tan version of my suitcase, without the neon-pink ribbon around it. This was disappointing. This was a *new* building. It was concrete, unadorned, unexceptional. How would I find any gems and nuggets for my Mental Pool staying in a building that looked like a plain paper bag?

"Righteous," said Bonnie, who had a deep appreciation for the humble and understated.

Charlotte had her nose buried in the information packet and did not comment. Without looking up, she stepped sideways to avoid a ball Chaz had thrown to Bud.

"Shouldn't there be a bellboy or something? Don't they have those here?" Janet asked, squinting up at the building as the bus driver hurled our suitcases onto the sidewalk with the force of a world-class wrestler.

"Now, now, Janet," I said severely. "We are in Paree. Do you dare question *les Français*?" Because it was one thing for me to question our accommodations. But another thing for Janet to do it.

"It's Jah-nay," she replied, trying not to scowl.

Madame Chavotte was making a clucking noise, trying to gather us around her. The noise she was making seemed more likely to attract eight chickens than eight almost-ninth graders. Bud and Chaz were still playing catch, but Tim had materialized beside Madame Chavotte silently, like Death wielding his scythe. Lewis ambled over without looking up from his Sidekick. Charlotte took my arm and led me with determination to the group. Sometimes having Charlotte as my best friend is like having a bodyguard/personal manager with an exceptionally high IQ.

"Ecoutez, mes enfants," Madame Chavotte said in her booming voice. It was physically impossible NOT to *écoutez* to Madame Chavotte when she spoke this loudly. My eardrums were convulsing with the trauma.

"Eet ees now"—and she briefly checked her watch—"twelve o'clock, Paree time. For you zees ees six in ze morning, New York time. We must dispense wiz ze jet lag *immédiatement* because starting tomorrow, our schedule ees very beezee. Ze concierge will direct boys to boys' dormitory and girls to girls' dormitory, and you will pliz nap or rest quietly until dinner."

Dormitory?

DORMITORY?

"Dormitory?" I asked. "I need to be able to describe the life of quiet elegance, exquisite simplicity, and unquestionably good taste. How am I going to find that in a dormitory?"

But Madame Chavotte was already sweeping through

 24

the door, waving at us to follow.

I turned pleadingly to Charlotte as we walked inside.

"*Dormitory?*"

Charlotte shrugged.

"Lily, this isn't a Lizzie McGuire movie; it's real life. We're fourteen. We don't *get* four-star accommodations."

"It's cool," said Bonnie, staring up at the giant tan suitcase with her pale-blue eyes. "It's like a youth hostel, man."

A youth hostile? That sounded to me like an angry, mean place to be avoided.

The lobby, if that's what you called it (Janet was temporarily without a Francophile contribution), was dark, especially after we'd been standing in the bright August sun. I could see a small man scurrying around, discharging rapid bursts of French in Madame Chavotte's direction. Our luggage had already been whisked away by a slightly larger man.

"*Pour les filles, deuxième étage; pour les garçons, troisième étage,*" the concierge was saying.

I was momentarily thunderstruck. I HAD UNDERSTOOD HIM!

"Girls, second floor; boys, third floor!" I shrieked excitedly, as if I'd just answered the Daily Double on *Jeopardy*. "Girls, second floor; boys, third floor!"

Our group was trooping dutifully up the staircase. No

one was responding with the astonishment I had expected following my remarkable translation of the concierge's directions. But it didn't matter. I was just grateful we were on the second floor. That meant only one flight of stairs. Because to be brutally honest (which is what writers must be), I could possibly stand to get in a little better shape. I could, perhaps, benefit from some close personal interaction with a treadmill. You get my drift.

So imagine my horror when we reached the first landing and the concierge KEPT GOING.

"*Deuxième étage* for the girls, *deuxième étage!*" I said, pointing frantically.

"*Oui, mademoiselle, deuxième étage,*" the concierge agreed cheerfully, trudging up the next flight of stairs.

"He's taking" (breath) "us past" (breath) "our floor" (breath), I gasped.

Through half-closed eyes, I saw something whiz through the air. It was Janet's ponytail as she whirled around to face me.

"In France the street level is called the *rez-de-chaussée*," she said primly. "The next level up is the *premier étage*. And so on."

Which makes *deuxième* the THIRD floor! Ye gads!

Ahead, Bud and Chaz were tripping up the stairs lightly while carrying on a nonstop conversation about the start of football season, in which neither one paused to listen to the other. Even Lewis, who as a Computer Geek should by all rights have the muscular and aerobic capacity of an earthworm, had enough surplus energy to enable him to continue web surfing while stair climbing.

Perhaps it was not too late for me to catch the bus back to the airport.

"*Voilà! Deuxième étage!*" said the concierge.

"*Allez,* girls, come wiz me. Monsieur Bellhomme will show ze boys upstairs."

Never had the voice of Madame Chavotte sounded more appealing. I staggered through the door, gasping and clutching at my chest theatrically.

"Don't bury yourself in the part," Charlotte remarked.

Madame Chavotte led us to a large room at the end of the hall. Shortly after ordering us to unpack before napping, she disappeared. I have no idea where she went. It occurred to me she might have stepped through a wardrobe and ended up in a French version of Narnia.

Our dormitory looked like the one in Miss Clavel's school, proving once again that everything you need to know about Paris can be found in the Madeline books. There were eight beds, in two rows of four. Next to each bed was a little wardrobe. I took the bed closest to the door, not because I felt it had any particular advantage over the others, but because it required the fewest steps to reach. Bonnie and Charlotte took the next two beds. Janet, for some reason probably related to French customs, took a bed in the facing row, off in the corner.

I plunged facedown on the bed and lay still, practicing what one of my favorite writers calls prone yoga. I could hear Charlotte unpacking with ruthless efficiency, hanging and folding clothes with military precision.

"You should unpack right now," Charlotte said, "so the wrinkles come out of your clothes. You should always unpack first thing when arriving in a new place. It's one of those rules for how to be a more efficient person."

Without removing my face from where it was pressed into the pillow, I made a small noise that sounded like a lamb bleating through many layers of gauze wrapping.

"And what about your journal? If you don't write things while they're fresh in your mind, you may forget important details," Charlotte continued.

Ye gads! She was right. I had an OFFICIAL DUTY to perform. Madame Chavotte wanted me to publish my Parisian journal in our school paper, in installments, for the edification and amusement of the unlucky masses who had not accompanied us. For this I would receive a coveted Extra Credit for French class. My Parisian journal would be read only by the school, but it would pave the way for my Great Parisian Novel, which would naturally be read by the World.

I lifted my head, which now felt more like a bowling ball, and struggled to a sitting position.

Must. Write. Now.

FROM THE PARISIAN DIARY OF
Lily M. Blennerhassett

We have arrived! We are all practically giddy with excitement. Paris is abuzz with energy. Refreshed and invigorated after our flight, we are ready to sink our teeth into the City of Lights, and what could be a better way than with our first real French meal—shortly to be served at our very own cozy home away from home, the Ville Ecole Internationale. Bon appétit indeed!

Three hours later I was half dead from sleep. The little nap did nothing to improve my jet lag; in fact, it seemed to have made it worse. I looked like I had a leech stuck under each eye. Our whole group was zonked. We'd shuffled into the dining hall like a collection of extras from *Dawn of the Dead*.

The dining room was arranged in picnic-table style. I slid onto a bench between Bonnie and Charlotte and discreetly checked my shirt for drool. Janet sat down across the table from me, practically quivering with excitement. Let her not speak, O Powers That Be. PLEASE. Let her not speak.

"Bon appétit, girls!" Janet sang.

"Technically, one doesn't say that until the food has been served and eating is about to commence," said Charlotte.

"What do you think they'll be feeding us to inaugurate our European palates?" Janet asked. *"Steak au poivre? Escargots? Pommes de terre? Terrine de—de . . ."*

We were spared any more of Janet's musings by the arrival of Madame Chavotte, pushing a wheeled trolley full of plates.

"Voilà! Voici!" she said, handing us each a steaming plate. "Take."

In spite of the Supreme Irritation Known as Janet and Her Enthusiasm, I was eager to see what we were having. The entire world has heard tales of the magical French cuisine. These would be the first items for my Mental Pool! I could have a sumptuous dining scene in my novel, with realistic descriptions of every course. I looked expectantly at my plate.

It was franks and beans.

"Hey. HEY! What IS this?" I demanded.

"Franks and beans," said Charlotte.

"That was a RHETORICAL question," I spluttered.

"Are you going to eat that?"

Charlotte had already taken a bite of her frank, word-lessly answering my question.

"Bonnie, are you?" I asked. And I glanced over at her plate. Then I went white with rage. (Okay, I didn't go white with rage, but it sounds good, doesn't it? One day I plan to go white with rage.) What I actually did was make a little envious, frustrated exclamatory sound. Kind of like "whahuh?!"

Because Bonnie didn't have franks and beans on her plate. She had what very closely resembled steamed veg-etables, sliced hard-boiled egg, soybeans, and rice. She had, in other words, something that looked . . . good. Not necessarily French, but possibly novelworthy. And definitely tasty.

"But . . . ," I said.

"I'm a vegetarian, dude, remember?" Bonnie said. "So they don't serve me the same thing they serve you."

"There was a box to check on the form that came in the information packet, Lily," said Charlotte. She had a tiny sliver of baked bean stuck on her lower lip. I was feel-ing mean, so I didn't tell her.

"Well, I've been giving it a lot of THOUGHT," I exclaimed, "and I have decided to become a vegetarian. As of right now."

"Bud, that's EXCELLENT," said Bonnie, beaming.

"So I will accept my vegetarian meal now," I said primly.

"It doesn't work that way," Charlotte said. "You have to tell them when you register. You can't change without rendering due notice."

The piece of bean was still stuck to her lip.

I sighed and picked up my fork.

"I am currently, but perhaps temporarily, once again a meat-atarian," I said. I took a bite of my dinner. "But I do think they MIGHT have been a little more . . . *French* with the meal."

"I agree!" exclaimed Janet.

"Oh, come on," said Charlotte cheerfully. "When you get right down to it, there's really nothing more French than a frank."

I wasn't in the mood for Charlotte's sophisticated, cultural wordplay.

But between you and me, Dear Readers, it was the best frank I'd ever tasted.

Three

Madame Chavotte woke us at seven thirty the next morning, making me feel like one of those army trainees awakening in the barracks at dawn to a barrage of commands from a towering military figure. We had to make our beds, but no one was ordered to do push-ups or clean the toilets with a toothbrush.

Any hopes for a traditional French breakfast were shattered with the arrival of a collection of cereal boxes and pitchers of milk. There was also a stack of sliced bread piled precariously next to an industrial-size toaster. But the light at the end of the tunnel was the discovery of the only valid item of European cuisine to be found within fifty feet of the VEI—a jar of Nutella. Nutella: bliss in a thirteen-ounce spreadable form. Nutella: my current *raison d'être*. Quite simply, it's chocolate hazelnut paste. You spread it on bread and eat it. This is essentially like having a piping-hot piece of toast with chocolate frosting smeared on top. And this is not even considered nutritionally warped behavior in Paris; in fact, it is as normal as tucking into a bowl of granola and milk. Chocolate paste on toast. Now *there's* something to inspire a writer.

I love Paris! *J'aime Nutella!*

Madame Chavotte wanted to start our first morning in Paris with Something Big, leading us with a purposeful stroll over the Pont Neuf to Notre Dame Cathedral. Bud and Chaz were high-fiving each other and whooping the whole way, because apparently there is a football team called Notre Dame, and they thought we were going to see a game.

When we arrived, we gathered on the square in front of the cathedral, where the massive towers loomed over us. Lewis and the Mysterious Tim stood lurking silently in their black T-shirts, looking like a team of junior Secret Service agents. At this point even Bud's and Chaz's teeny brains figured out we were definitely *not* at a sports arena. Bud (or it might have been Chaz) then had a shining intellectual moment when, recovering from his disappointment, he pointed a beefy finger at the cathedral and said, "Hey! It's that church from the Disney movie!"

Charlotte shook her head in disgust.

"This cathedral has been standing for seven hundred years and is considered the crowning Gothic architectural masterpiece of the world," she said. "And Bud only knows it from the cartoon version of *The Hunchback of Notre Dame*."

"Disgraceful!" I agreed. It was the sort of thing only a Very Simple Tourist would have known: a Disney fact.

"LISTEN, PLIZ!" Madame Chavotte was calling. She might be the only human being in the world who sounded like she was using a megaphone when she wasn't. Really, how could a person NOT listen?

"You 'ave read ze information sheet on ze 'istory of ze cassedral, which also 'as a map on ze uzzer side. So I sink is good for you to explore ze cassedral *seuls*. Okay? Good? *Seuls*."

Good soul? Was there some sort of spiritual requirement to get in? Was my soul good? If it wasn't, would I be sent down a hatch like Veruca Salt in *Charlie and the Chocolate Factory*? I envisioned standing on a platform at the cathedral's entrance, and a sign lighting up, blinking on and off "BAD SOUL." Criminy!

"Can they do that?" I whispered anxiously to Charlotte.

"Do what?" she asked.

"Evaluate our souls?"

Charlotte stared at me with her eyebrows all squinched together.

"Lily, what are you talking about?"

I pulled her away from the group and whispered, "Madame Chavotte said that to go into the cathedral, we needed good soul!"

Charlotte covered her face with her hands. I could hear a muffled sigh of frustration.

"Didn't you study any French vocabulary before this trip?" she asked through her hands.

"Uh, some," I said. *"Oui."*

I *had* studied my vocabulary words. It's just that my brain retained only words that seemed important to me, personally. Like *écrivain*. After all, what could be more important than the French word for "writer"?

"She said she thought it would be good *seuls*, Lily. *Seuls*. Alone. She thinks it would be fun for us to explore the cathedral on our own."

YAY! My soul was not going to be evaluated!

"Oh, right," I said casually. "*Seuls*. Right. It's the jet lag."

Charlotte was polite enough not to respond to that lie.

"This is excellent, bros," Bonnie said. She had been staring, transfixed, at the cathedral since we'd arrived. This was the first time she'd spoken. "There are going to be some massively good vibrations in there. I'm going to go find a quiet spot and attune my consciousness." She began walking toward the cathedral. Actually, she looked more like a disembodied spirit, gliding over the paving stones, all delicate and mystical.

My consciousness could probably use a tune-up too, but I didn't really know how to go about doing that. Not only could I not locate the information sheet Madame Chavotte had given us, but I hadn't bothered to read it before I lost it. Rats. This meant I didn't have the map either.

"Do you have the map?" I asked Charlotte, giving her a wide and innocent smile.

Charlotte looked stern.

"Where's your— Oh, never mind. We'll explore the cathedral *seules* together."

I hugged her and saw a pleased twinkle behind her stern expression.

"But you have *got* to get more organized," Charlotte said as we walked toward the cathedral with our arms linked.

"I will," I said.

And we went inside.

As a writer I am ashamed, ASHAMED, to admit it, but it is difficult to find the words to describe what I felt when I stepped into Notre Dame Cathedral. It was like suddenly finding oneself at the bottom of a spectacular ocean. There was a sense of hugeness. The vaulted ceiling was so high, it seemed like an optical illusion. The altar at the far end of the cathedral looked miles away. Everything was so big: the pillars, the stained glass windows.

I felt positively puny.

It was also strangely quiet. There were noises—I could hear other people and stuff—but everything was sort of muffled. Even the air felt quiet, and . . . *smoother*. Maybe it was those massively good vibrations Bonnie had mentioned.

We don't have much Really Old Stuff in the U.S. Our ancient historical sites are more of the Laura Ingalls Wilder variety. But the Little House on the Prairie was an architectural infant in diapers compared to this. Some person—a girl my age, even—might have stood on this EXACT spot seven hundred years ago. Looking at the EXACT same thing I was looking at now. My mind sagged trying to get around the idea.

Charlotte tugged my arm, and I stifled a shriek of alarm.

"Come on," she whispered. "I want to see the Le Brun paintings and the rose windows."

I followed Charlotte as we strolled past Lewis, who was fiddling with his Sidekick while standing next to a statue of someone very pure and holy-looking. Charlotte led me by the paintings down to an enormous circle of stained glass. She occasionally whispered to me (everyone seemed to speak in hushed tones here), but I had trouble focusing on anything she was saying. We must have wandered for an hour, Charlotte pointing out statues and carved screens. I was actually beginning to regret not reading the information sheet as the Simple Tourists had. Because I didn't know what anything was, and now that I was here, I couldn't retain the information Charlotte was giving me. I was hypnotized by the stone, by the greatness, by the age. By Bonnie's massively good vibrations.

Plus, I was really jet-lagged.

Still, I took something away with me when we left Notre Dame. It wasn't a specific gem or nugget I could identify for my Mental Pool. I just felt . . . refreshed. Maybe my consciousness had been tuned up without my even trying.

On the way back to the VEI, Madame Chavotte had us stop in the Place des Vosges, a square that surrounded a tree-lined garden with a fountain in the middle. She had indicated through a series of barks and hand gestures that we should stretch our legs, window-shop at the street-level boutiques, or park it on a bench for the next hour. Charlotte paced the entire perimeter of the square, looking for a news shop that sold *The Economist*. Bonnie found a quiet, shady spot on the grass and was sitting in the lotus position. She looked like Siddhartha sitting under a Bodhi tree awaiting enlightenment.

I parked it on a bench beside Lewis, who had also parked it on a bench. Curious, I peered at him out of the corner of my eye. He had flipped open his Sidekick. Again.

"I don't get it," I said.

"Don't get what?" Lewis asked, fingers already tapping at buttons.

"All this technology you're so hooked on. You're in PARIS! Why miss it all while you bury your nose in the computer screen?"

Lewis looked at me blankly. I tried again.

"My parents took me to New York City for a weekend last summer," I said. "They had this whole museum agenda, part of their Frequent Outings Program to torture and traumatize me, but that's another story. Anyway, we kept seeing these double-decker tour buses go by, like down Fifth Avenue, and all the people on the top deck were filming with their video cameras. They're riding right by Rockefeller Center and St. Patrick's Cathedral and all these tourist landmarks, and most of them never took their eyes out of the viewfinders. It's like they were so intent on videotaping every last second of their vacation, they were essentially experiencing the whole trip through a lens. Might just as well have stayed home and watched a TV show about New York, don't you think?"

Lewis waited a moment, to make sure I was finished talking.

 40

"Is that what you think I'm doing?" he asked.

"You web surf, like, twenty-four/seven."

"No, I don't. I text message every once in a while and post updates on my blog—"

"Blog?" I asked. "You have a blog?"

"—and there are some sites I check every day. But at breakfast, for instance, I was looking at this."

Lewis turned the Sidekick to face me. On the screen was a series of drawings of the Place des Vosges, from the time of its construction in the seventeeth century to the present day.

"Where did you find that?" I asked.

"I Googled it," Lewis said. "It shows how the Place des Vosges is completely symmetrical. Nine houses on each side. The square could be bisected from any angle and still produce twin images, the perfection of bilateral symmetry. Humans are attracted to bilateral symmetry. That's a biological fact."

I absorbed this information with my mouth hanging open.

"You see," Lewis continued, "technology doesn't have to be a mindless escape, Lily. It can enhance an experience. You're just prejudiced because you're a writer, and writers consider the Internet beneath them."

I was thrilled both that Lewis had (accurately) referred to me as a writer and that he thought I had a big enough ego to consider anything "beneath me."

"I don't think I'm above it, or anything," I said quickly. "Maybe it's just my genes. I come from, like, the least technologically savvy family since the Flintstones. We don't have DSL. We didn't even have Internet access until a year ago, when my dad needed to read his office e-mail from home. And if my mother didn't entertain these recurrent terrifying fantasies that I was going to get Separated from the Group on this trip, she never in a blue moon would have bought me a cell phone."

"Show me," said Lewis.

I groped around in my bag until I found it. Then I silently handed it over to Lewis, who flipped it open and scrutinized it.

"Nice one. You can text message on this," Lewis said. "And take pictures. It's a good phone."

"I don't know how to text message," I said.

"It's easy," Lewis replied. He started pushing buttons on the phone, which chirped back at him in a friendly way. "Okay, I just entered my e-mail address in your address book. So you down-arrow-key to 'write text message,' then highlight my address from the address book. After you've finished writing, just hit 'send.'"

"Well," I said, taking my phone back, "that's great, thank you, Lewis. But I'm not much of a correspondent, text message–wise."

In reality, the only person I would ever want to text message was Jake, and I didn't even know if his phone could do that. But I didn't mean to sound ungrateful.

"Thanks for showing me how it works, though," I added.

Lewis shrugged. "Just thought you should know how to use what you've got."

"Anything on the Internet about Lindy Sloane?" I asked, switching the subject. When Lewis didn't answer right away, I clarified.

"Lindy Sloane, the Singer/Actress/Celebrity Personality?"

Lewis studied me for a moment, the way he might look at an entirely new species of rodent discovered in Laos. Curious, but not necessarily in a good way. Maybe he didn't know who Lindy Sloane was.

"Please don't tell me you're one of those deluded Sloane fans," he said.

So he DID know who she was!

"The Sloane Rangers, you mean," I said.

Lewis nodded and pulled back slightly, as if he'd just realized I very possibly had the bubonic plague. Sloane Rangers lived and breathed for Lindy Sloane. They wore what she wore (or cheap knockoffs). They ate what she ate. They read what she claimed to be reading. And they spent every second of their free time in Lindy Sloane chat rooms, posting articles and fanfic on Lindy Sloane forums, and poring over the latest paparazzi pics posted on the gossip sites.

"No, Lewis, I am not a Sloane Ranger. In fact, I am imperatively, aggressively, and categorically NOT a Sloane Ranger. You might say I'm the anti–Sloane Ranger. I consider myself more of a Celebrity Social Crime Scene Analyst. I keep track of the outrageous antics, and I incorporate them into the Character Portion of my Mental Pool."

"Your Mental Pool?" asked Lewis. He still looked a bit worried about bubonic contagion.

"It's a writer thing." I said.

"Uh-huh," Lewis said.

"And one of the people I constantly update in my Mental Pool is Lindy Sloane. In case I ever want to write a novel satirizing Hollywood." Because she certainly wasn't going to make it into my Great Parisian Novel. Lindy Sloane and Paris went together like oil and water. Like chocolate and mayonnaise. Like Not at All.

Lewis stared at me for a while, like he was still trying to decide if helping someone who admittedly had a Mental Pool was ethical or dangerous. After about a minute he hit a few keys on his Sidekick and read from the screen.

"She's gone platinum," he said.

"Her CD!" I cried, stunned.

"Her hair," Lewis said. "Platinum blond. They say she

44

might have also added some extensions."

Now Lindy Sloane as a platinum blonde was just wrong, wrong, wrong. She had been a redhead forever.

But I waited for Lewis to continue.

"She's missed a few days of work filming *Space Teen*. Her publicist said she had the flu and got dehydrated, but a source close to the film crew says she just ran off without telling anybody."

I nodded shrewdly, as any person does when a publicist says a star "got the flu."

"The publicist says she's on location but needs to recover from exhaustion."

I nodded again.

"That's about all," Lewis said. "There are some quotes from the *Space Teen* cast saying the usual things: Lindy is the hardest-working girl in Hollywood, she does eat, and she isn't too skinny, she just photographs that way—that kind of stuff."

"Thanks, Lewis," I said sincerely. "I guess I came down too hard on your Sidekick."

I have to say, seeing Lewis in the summer Paris light, outlined with leaves and the elegant buildings of the Place des Vosges in the background, I realized that he looked . . . even smaller and younger than I'd always thought. He probably wouldn't be a bad-looking guy, in twenty years or so, especially to women of the five-foot-three-and-under set. But right now he just looked like a very small guy whose eyes and nose were too big for his face. Still, he was trying to be nice to me. And he'd given me the Lindy Sloane update. I wouldn't forget that.

Suddenly Charlotte appeared out of nowhere, looking distraught and out of sorts.

"What's wrong?" I asked quickly. Had she been robbed? Insulted? Had Charlotte been arrested?

"I've checked every shop here, and I can't find *one* that has the latest edition of *The Economist*!" she cried.

"So you'll find it tomorrow," I said.

Charlotte appeared, at this moment, to turn legitimately white with rage.

"The issue is published TODAY," she said. "I need to read it TODAY. While the news is still FRESH and CURRENT."

"There might be an online version," Lewis said. "Maybe I can access it."

Charlotte looked at Lewis as if he had just pulled a family of puppies from a burning building. After just a few taps he turned the screen toward Charlotte. From where I was sitting, I could see the red rectangular logo of *The Economist* on the screen.

Charlotte gave a little shriek of delight and instantly began to read.

Paris really has brought out the best in Lewis.

Today was a stroll to the magical Gothic world of Notre Dame Cathedral! With the appropriate scholastic preparation, 700 years of history simply sprang to life before me! My exhaustive knowledge of French medieval architecture certainly served me well. I might have waxed philosophical over flying buttresses all day had we not been required to stretch our legs in the direction of the Place des Vosges. After such a day immersed in antiquity and artistic genius, our modern-day culture is all but forgotten!

Four

I have stated More Than Once that I am no Simple
Tourist. So you can imagine the shock, the DISMAY
I felt when I learned what was on the board for the
day. I found out by asking Charlotte, the Information
Pack Commando, as we ate our Very Not French break-
fast that morning.

"Don't you have your schedule, Lily?" Charlotte asked.
"Where's your information pack?"

"I left it in the thingy," I said casually.

"What thingy?"

"Charlotte, you have yours IN YOUR HAND. It's just
a simple question! What are we doing today?"

Charlotte was taking longer than usual to be mollified.

"You should already know," she said.

Arghhh.

"I did know, Charlotte. But I've FORGOTTEN."

"Lily, you must become more detail oriented!" Charlotte said, waving her rolled-up copy of the schedule around like a broadsword.

I never could understand why Charlotte, who knew me better than anyone, had never grasped the simple fact that writers are the ONE group of people on earth who should not have to be bothered with things like DETAILS. Had I not just the past year had a job as an Assistant to a Real Writer, dealing with little irritants like crumbs and Post-its? Did this not prove that Real Writers could not deal with these little things themselves? Did Charles Dickens concern himself with printed itineraries and street maps while writing *Oliver Twist*? I think not.

"Can you just tell me where we're going, Charlotte?" I asked meekly.

Charlotte produced one of her vintage sighs.

"Disneyland," she replied.

"Very funny," I said. "Where are we going today?"

Charlotte stared at me evenly.

"Disneyland," she repeated.

It was even less funny the second time.

"Fine. I apologize for not being detail oriented enough and vow to do better in the future. There, I've said it. Okay? Now where are we going?"

"Disneyland Paris."

O Hammer of Thor! She was SERIOUS! You can't expect a writer to visit Disneyland while in Paris. That was like expecting Mozart to compose while listening to Snoop Doggy Dogg. That was like asking van Gogh to paint under a strobe light. Like wanting the Dalai Lama to meditate while bungee jumping. THERE WOULD BE NO GEMS AND NUGGETS FOR MY MENTAL POOL IN DISNEYLAND PARIS!

"Okay, wait," I said. "Charlotte, it has to be a mistake. You and I both know our parents didn't cough up the Benjamins for this trip so we could go to Disneyland. This is supposed to be educational."

"Remember the orientation meeting for this trip?" Charlotte asked.

I feared I was being lured into a trap, but I nodded. I did remember.

"Remember whose dad made the trip possible by getting our group the fifty-eight-percent discount on plane fare?"

"Yeah, it was Bud's dad. Or Chaz's dad. One of them."

"That's right. And what company does Bud's dad have the special work connection with, that he told us all about?"

Crapstick. I had tried to jettison this information into a Memory Abyss, but now it was bubbling back to the surface.

"Walt Disney," I mumbled.

"And what did Bud's dad really, *really* want us to do in Paris since we were flying on his discount?"

"Visit Disneyland Paris," I muttered.

"As his complimentary guests."

"As his complimentary guests," I repeated. Okay, in a dog-eat-dog world it made sense. When offered hugely discounted plane tickets, Madame Chavotte and our parents could not very well look a gift horse in the mouth and refuse the additional "offer" of free admission to Disneyland Paris. But surely there would be some kind of loud, unarmed rebellion? Certainly we did not intend to go quietly into that good fright?

"Bonnie? Do you realize we have to go to Disneyland today?" I asked.

Bonnie was gazing dreamily into her mug of green tea.

"Yeah, man, of course! I've always wanted to see Sleeping Beauty's Castle."

Bonnie, Goddess of the New Age, Channeler of Universal Intent, Communicator with Angels, had always wanted to get closer to . . . Sleeping Beauty's personal residence?

"Janet?" I asked. She looked up from the Paris guidebook she was immersed in.

"*J'aime bien le* Teacup Ride!" she squealed. "Is it time to go?"

I was outnumbered. I was defeated. Unless I developed a sudden case of appendicitis, à la Madeline, I was going to Disneyland Paris. The Land of the Wee and the Home of the Knave. Realm of the Simple Tourist.

Oh. The Humanity.

EVERYTHING YOU EVER WANTED TO KNOW ABOUT
DISNEYLAND PARIS BUT WERE AFRAID TO ASK,
ACCORDING TO LILY M. BLENNERHASSETT:

MOST VOMITATIOUS RIDE: Space Mountain

BEST INSTANT CONNECTION TO CHILDHOOD:
Bonnie running toward Captain Hook's Pirate
Ship in a decidedly Tinkerbellian fashion

BEST PICTURE: Charlotte clapping hands over
eyes outside Phantom Manor and feigning horror

WORST SCHEDULING DECISION: Consumption of
chili dog and extra-large fries twenty minutes
prior to boarding Indiana Jones and the Temple
of Peril Ride

MOST EMBARRASSING MOMENT: Too many to specify

NUMBER OF SLOANE RANGERS SPOTTED: Nine

LEAST USEFUL ARTICLE ACQUIRED: Three-foot-high
stuffed Donald Duck won at arcade by Lewis

INTELLECTUAL PEAK: Spontaneously recalling seven miscellaneous facts about the Gold Rush while strolling through Frontierland

TIMES SEPARATED FROM GROUP: None!

NUTRITIONAL ACCOMPLISHMENT: Consuming Mickey Mouse–shaped lollipop measuring nine inches in diameter in under seven minutes

VISITS TO LADIES' ROOM: Fourteen (three for hand and face washing only)

FRENCH WORDS SPOKEN: One (if "ooh-la-la" counts)

MOST IRRITATING INCIDENT: Janet insisting on calling Sleeping Beauty's Castle *Le Château de la Belle au Bois Dormant*

MOST TERRIFYING SIGHT: Bud and Chaz trying to flirt with Snow White

MOST SOBERING MOMENT: Madame Chavotte boarding the Dumbo ride behind Tim

IMPORTANT LIFE LESSONS LEARNED: See "Worst Scheduling Decision"

PARISIAN GEMS AND NUGGETS RECORDED: Zero

I dozed off once or twice during the train ride back to Paris. Jet lag, it turns out, has absolutely NOTHING on Disney lag. For someone who'd allegedly spent the entire day in recreational activities, I felt like a swimmer who'd just doggy-paddled across the English Channel. My overfed stomach was pooching out against the waistband of my jeans like I'd swallowed a beach ball. At least Jake wasn't around to see that. My feet throbbed. My eardrums hurt. And I seem to have left my sense of balance back on Space Mountain, because every time I closed my eyes, I felt my head spin.

But I will admit in secret, Dear Readers, that I kind of enjoyed myself.

Janet was chattering away to Bonnie, who was listening with what appeared to me to be a Profound Level of Tolerance. Charlotte had somehow acquired a copy of *The Wall Street Journal*, but she seemed to be finished reading it. At least I assumed that was the reason she was holding the paper on her lap and staring at me for great lengths of time.

"What?" I asked her. "Did I fall asleep again? Oh, God, was I drooling?"

"No drool," Charlotte replied.

Yay!

"So what's on the books for tomorrow? No wax museums or Hard Rock Cafe, I hope. I can't handle any more of the Simple Tourist Life. My stomach is about to explode!"

"I worry about you, Lily," Charlotte said.

There is little worse in life than when your best friend starts channeling your mother.

"Is this about the chili dog and the lollipop? Because I'm really fine now. Honest."

"I'm serious," Charlotte said.

Of course she was. Charlotte was always serious.

"Why would you be worried about me?" I asked.

"Because, Lily Blennerhasset, you're scatterbrained. You aren't always going to have a personal assistant to fill you in on what's happening. Your life isn't always going to have easy-to-read instructions printed on the side of the box. Take a little control over the details of your life. You'll need them when you've become a Great Writer."

"Is that all? Jeez, Charlotte, you scared me for a minute. I thought maybe I had a new nose growing out of the back of my head, or something."

"It's never too soon to start, Lily. Read a map. Reference a guidebook. Locate your information pack."

I gave Charlotte my brightest smile. "When I could never possibly improve upon the organizational skills of my best friend, the keen and coolly brilliant Charlotte McGrath, Future Corporate Executive and World Leader, who is always at my side?"

Charlotte just shook her head.

"But that's the thing, Lily. I *won't* always be at your side."

"Are we talking about college? Because that's YEARS away," I said. "Besides which, I still think we stand a very good chance of finding a college that offers both a world-class corporate education AND an outstanding creative writing program. We'll be roommates!"

Charlotte smiled.

"That would be cool, Lily. But what if we're not? You have to stop relying on me so much. I don't mean to hurt your feelings, but you *flounder* when I'm not around. Or worse. Remember when I went away to Young Executive Camp last summer? You were on your own for what, three weeks? And what happened?"

Oh, come on. It wasn't THAT bad. There was that little problem with hotel security, true. There was at some point police involvement. And, okay, there was the lawsuit, and the depositions, and the attorneys. Some trouble with inappropriate credit card use. Oh yeah, and a brush with Blennerhasset Bankruptcy and Ruination. But then everything got fixed. Around the time . . . around the time that Charlotte came home.

It was obviously time for an Abrupt Subject Change.

"I totally forgot to ask how your Unilever stock was doing!" I exclaimed.

Charlotte had purchased some stock with her own money and passionately followed its ups and downs in the newspaper. It was a subject we both knew perfectly well she could not resist discussing. And technically it was a Detail. I had Oriented a Detail.

"Well, actually, I was just reading about that," Charlotte said, rattling her *Wall Street Journal* for emphasis. "The effect of corn growth on the world market just boggles the mind."

I listened with enthusiasm, though Charlotte's animated discussion of the impact of rainfall on long-term interest rates was something we both knew I could never even vaguely understand. Instead, I just enjoyed watching Charlotte in her element. I didn't need to be able to understand the stock market to know how smart Charlotte was. I didn't need to know what a pork belly future was to see that Charlotte already knew what she wanted to do in life, that she was going to be aces at it, and that her work would make her happy.

How I admire Charlotte McGrath.

Through the window I could see French things speeding by in a blur. The sun was low in the sky. I realized once again how thoroughly exhausted I was. And absolutely no closer to beginning the Great Parisian Novel. Maybe tomorrow I would find some gems and nuggets. I realized Charlotte hadn't answered my questions about our upcoming agenda, so I still had no idea where we were going tomorrow. But I certainly wasn't going to ask Charlotte again. She was positively glowing after her analysis of the effect of corn products on Unilever's stock price. Tomorrow would just have to be a surprise. I'd follow everybody like I always do, and when we got where we were going, I'd know where we were.

Really, what could be simpler?

FROM THE PARISIAN DIARY OF
Lily M. Blennerhassett

Ah, Paris. How like a carnival! How it leaves one feeling giddy and breathless as a child!

Five

As it turned out, I didn't need Charlotte for information about what the next day had in store for us. Madame Chavotte paid us a visit in our room before breakfast and told us repeatedly that she had booked us on a group tour at Paris's most famous museum, the Louvre, beginning at one P.M. sharp. Yay! Educational, and GUARANTEED to provide gems and nuggets! Although having not read the sheet in the information packet, I could only assume this to be the case.

We would have the morning to ourselves and would be permitted to explore our neighborhood WITH THE STRICT PROVISION that we remain all together or in two groups, boys and girls. No one, for any reason, was to become Separated from the Group. We were to take the bus or the metro to the museum, using the map and directions provided in our information packets. Or in my case, the map and directions provided in Charlotte's information packet. There we would assemble by what Madame Chavotte called "ze glesspairmeed," which both Charlotte and Janet claimed to understand. Because of what Charlotte had said on the train last night, I didn't ask her what "ze glesspairmeed" was. I didn't want another lecture. All would become known to me in good time, I figured. Like Bonnie always said, the Universe revealed everything to us when we most needed it.

We were standing outside the VEI as Madame Chavotte reviewed the instructions for the fourth time. She had intensified her tone so that she sounded more like she was auditioning for a yodeling contest than performing her chaperoning duties.

"Okay, zen, if you MUST spleet up, you go in TWO GROUPS ONLY. Ze boys wis ze boys, ze girls wis ze girls, *ça va*? Do NOT GET SEPARATED FROM ZE GROUP. Eet ees *absolument* forbeeden. Eef you break zis rule, forget eet. No more Paree. No more nussing! We will cancel everysing. No more treeps ever. *D'accord?* Good. Okay. At lunchtime, you are taking *le métro* or *le bus* to the Louvre, where we will all meet at ze glesspairmeed at exactly one P.M. *Comprenez?*"

Everyone nodded energetically. After yodeling the same

set of instructions one final time, Madame Chavotte reluctantly released us. As instructed, we separated into two groups and dispersed like a flock of carrier pigeons suddenly freed in the wild. Well, the girls did at least. I looked back to see the boys standing around, looking genuinely flummoxed. Bud and Chaz were taking tentative steps back and forth. Lewis, polishing his Sidekick case with his shirt, looked like he was trying to figure out a way to come with us. And the Mysterious Tim was missing altogether, the unfortunate victim, apparently, of a stomach virus. Or maybe he did the chili-dog-before-the-ride thing at Disneyland Paris too. Though I'd never even made eye contact with Tim (that I was aware of), I couldn't help feeling sorry for him—blowing chow on vacation in Paris. But Charlotte was already blazing a path down the street, and there was no time to offer them helpful suggestions. We had to take care of ourselves. Or rather, we had to let Charlotte take care of us. Which at this moment involved running down the street after her.

"Where are we going?" I called to Charlotte. I had to practically jog to catch up with her. Janet was plodding clumsily beside me, out of breath, but Bonnie had somehow managed to get way up ahead, drifting like a medieval apparition with her long, straw-colored hair streaming behind her.

"You absolutely *must* see Victor Hugo's house, Lily,"

Charlotte said, "and of course we can't miss the Pompidou. If we hurry, we might even have time to stop into the Musée Carnavalet before heading over to the Louvre."

It was really rather alarming how Charlotte knew about all these places, their hours of operation, and how to get there on foot. When Charlotte acted like this—like some kind of Madame-Chavotte-in-Training—I had to remember her loyalty, her sweetness, and her commitment to me. Even though she'd been positively parental with me last night, I knew that most of Charlotte's lectures were intended for the Benefit, Education, and Advancement of Lily M. Blennerhassett, a charity to which I myself was quite partial. Worry though she might, Charlotte believed in me. She believed I was a Great Writer, that I was going to become an even Greater Writer, and that I was fully capable of penning the Great Parisian Novel. Charlotte always stuck with me, through thick and thin. She helped me believe in myself. So if she was being kind of bossy, that was just fine with me.

Plus, I couldn't imagine ANYTHING more important, more inspiring, more legitimately Parisian than visiting the actual home of that genius *écrivain*, author of the masterpiece *Les Misérables*, Victor Hugo. It absolutely went without saying that the bona fide home of this Universally Acknowledged Literary Great would be bursting at the seams with gems and nuggets for my

Mental Pool. Just standing within those four walls, breathing that literary air, would probably inspire me to write the first sentence of my Great Parisian Novel!

I trotted alongside Charlotte happily, while Janet brought up the rear. But then we found ourselves deviating from the plan.

Charlotte started to cross the street, yet Bonnie was walking really fast—almost flying, in fact—down the Rue de Turenne. She looked, Dear Readers, like she was on a Mission from God.

"Bonnie! Bonnie, it's this way!" Charlotte called. Janet had caught up with us and was panting and heaving, muttering that we all walked *trop vite* and we needed to slow down a little and enjoy *la vie*. But there was no time to stand around gasping for air and listening to Janet itemize her complaints. Bonnie was a full block away and steaming ahead at full speed. If we didn't take off after her immediately, Bonnie would become Separated from the Group.

And that was not allowed.

So we went after her.

"*Je need rester!*" Janet was calling. "*Je veux* Diet Coke. . . ."

We made up a little ground when Bonnie had to pause at an intersection, but as we got closer, the light changed and she charged on. She seemed to be heading for the river. But then she made an abrupt turn down a curved street. By the time Charlotte and I reached the spot, we couldn't see Bonnie at all. We exchanged a quick look, ascertained (on the basis of the garbled fake-French–accented exclamations coming from that direction) that Janet was indeed behind us, then headed down the street where Bonnie had disappeared.

And came upon a vision.

It was as if Bonnie had walked right into a fairy tale. Directly in front of her was what looked like a small castle. But REAL. I mean, it put Sleeping Beauty's Castle to complete and utter shame. There were towers. There were arched windows. There was a massive Gothic doorway. All it lacked was Heath Ledger in a suit of armor atop a white stallion.

Bonnie was standing in front of the castle looking hypnotized. I know you're not supposed to disturb people who are sleepwalking, because you might startle them and they might accidentally attack you and yank your ears down below your waist. But I wasn't sure if the same thing held true for people who stood outside castles looking hypnotized. As a Writer I wanted to know immediately and in great detail what was going through Bonnie's mind, so I could add it to my Mental Pool. As a Human Being I was slightly freaked.

The dilemma was solved by Janet, still wheezing and

huffing and muttering about obtaining cold drinks. She marched up to Bonnie and tapped her sharply on the shoulder.

"Bonnie. Can we go now, *s'il vous plaît*? I have *le* thirst *terrible*."

Since Bonnie didn't rear back and swipe off Janet's head with her metro map, I cautiously approached her.

"Um . . . Bon? You okay?"

I have to say she looked okay. She was still staring at the castle, looking all golden and fresh like a daisy in a field. (Ew. Sorry for the oversentimentality.)

"I'm fine, man. I'm phat."

Janet made an explosive sound.

"You're not FAT, Bonnie. If anyone here needs to cut back a little on the carbs, it's—"

"What IS this place?" I asked, nodding toward the building.

"I used to live here," Bonnie said. She looked at me with a pleased smile, like she'd just worked out the theory of relativity all by herself, with a crayon on the back of a napkin.

"You used to live in PAREE?" cried Janet.

"What?" I added.

"When?" asked Charlotte, who was now exhibiting somewhat milder symptoms of hypnotization as she squinted up at the building.

"Three, maybe four hundred years ago," Bonnie said.

Charlotte, Janet, and I simultaneously paused with our mouths open in prequestion gape.

"Four hundred," Bonnie clarified, having been given some quiet time for thought.

"Wow," I said, trying to look casual and impressed at the same time. "Do they still forward your mail?"

Charlotte, meanwhile, was flipping rapidly through her guidebook.

"Okay, okay, here it is!" Charlotte said. "The Hôtel de Sens. It houses a fine-art collection. It was named for the archbishop of Sens."

"It's a hotel?" I asked. I couldn't help feeling disappointed. Bonnie lived in Paris four hundred years ago in a HOTEL?

"*Hôtel* can also mean private mansion or important building," Charlotte said. "It says the Hôtel de Sens is one of only three medieval-era residences left in the city."

I couldn't stop staring at Bonnie. And it wasn't just because she'd made this outrageous statement or led us straight through a city we'd never been in before directly to a building none of us, not even Charlotte, knew existed. I was staring at her because I believed her, and that might possibly indicate that I too had gone as nutty as a half-baked fruit loaf.

"I told you I had a past life in Paris," Bonnie said to me.

"I know," I said. "I just sort of thought it was . . . you know . . . a EUPHEMISM."

"It was built in 1475," Charlotte added.

"Are we going in?" I asked. Bonnie shook her head.

"Not necessary, man," she said. "I want to remember it the way it was. The past is past."

And then she turned and walked on, just like that.

"Finally!" Janet cried. "First café we see, we're stopping!"

"Lily," Charlotte whispered conspiratorially.

"What?" I whispered back.

Charlotte discreetly showed me a page of her guidebook, shielding it like it was a naughty magazine or a subversive publication.

"Look at this," she said.

The page was devoted to the Hôtel de Sens. It had a picture of the outside view and a few shots of the interior courtyard, which looked . . . well, medieval.

"Yeah, that's definitely the one," I said.

"No, here! This!" Charlotte whispered.

"In 1605 the first wife of Henri the Fourth, Queen Margot, lived in the Hôtel de Sens," I read.

"Shhh!"

Now I admit, math is not my strong point. But I realized what Charlotte was pointing out. The year 1605 was more or less four hundred years ago. Which might just make Bonnie . . . royalty.

Bonnie, once again, was in the lead.

"Follow that queen," I murmured.

We'd found a café with outdoor tables near the metro stop, and we were lounging back, our tummies bulging with pleasure. Janet had finally obtained her drink. After several futile attempts to communicate her desire for *un Coca diète,* the waiter finally inquired in perfectly good English if she meant a Coca Light.

In spite of the warm weather, Charlotte, Bonnie, and I had opted for what we'd heard was a fabled drink of mythical proportions: the French hot chocolate. We were rewarded for our daring by the appearance of three soup bowl–size servings of a deep brown liquid that seemed part drink, part meal. The first sip confirmed what we'd heard. I made a sound like a cat that had found a way into a fish market. Charlotte's eyes actually rolled back in her head. And Bonnie, whom I've seen looking peaceful more times than I can count, looked so serene, she appeared to be levitating several inches out of her chair. We were spoiled for life. We would never find satisfaction in powdered Nestlé's or Swiss Miss again. It is a moment I will remember until I take my last breath (which I may use asking for another French hot chocolate). I slurped desperately at the last dregs of chocolate, while Charlotte paid the bill (she was in charge of all Official French Transactions) and declared we needed to get going if were going to reach the Louvre on time.

But we were interrupted.

"Look!" Janet said, pointing. "Look at her, you guys. Look at that woman, right there!"

Janet was gesturing at a woman coming down the sidewalk with a tiny white dog. She didn't look like anything special to me—just a woman in a short skirt and a top that might be more appropriate for someone a tad younger. A decade or two.

"*That,*" whispered Janet reverently, "is a real *Parisienne.* Look at her posture! Those pearls! That outfit! Have you ever seen anything so chic? So sophisticated? So positively *formidable*? They simply do not make women like that in America. They simply do *not*. Edith Piaf could NEVER have been an American."

"Who is this Edith Piaf you keep going on about?" I asked.

But Janet was fixated on the approaching figure of alleged chicness. Oh, crapstick. It looked like Janet was going to try to TALK to the woman. The situation was morphing from Simply Stupid to Enormously Embarrassing. I thought about hiding under the table, but the quarters were too cramped. So I attempted to look like I didn't know Janet, like she'd just sat down with us accidentally. Then, to my horror, my fears were realized. Janet leaped up and extended a hand toward the woman.

"*Bonjour! Je m'appelle Jah-nay!*" she cried brightly.

"Watch the dawg—he bites," said the woman in a distinctly Long Island accent. "I don't speak French," she added, as an afterthought.

Now, I'm not all that fond of Janet, as you might have guessed. But even I felt a teeny bit bad for her when I saw her face collapse in disappointment.

"I thought . . . I thought . . . you were *French* . . . ," Janet stuttered.

The woman, who I could now see was actually CHEWING GUM, grinned.

"You ain't the only one, doll. I got the look down to my toes. Louis Vuitton," she said, patting her bag. "Chanel suit—*not* off the rack, mind you—cawst more than yaw fathah makes in a month. I only let Jean Louis David touch my hair. Shoes, of cawss, are Louboutin. And I'm sure you noticed my dawg's collar. Christian Lacroix! Cawst me nine hundred bucks! *That's* why you thought I was French, doll. I'm wearing thirty thousand dollahs' worth of the country as we speak!"

"Well, it's certainly . . . it's quite . . . chic," Janet said.

The woman pointed a manicured finger at her Chanel-encased torso.

"I speak chic, doll. I *am* chic." Then she tottered away on her improbably high heels. Janet looked thoroughly deflated.

But Charlotte was urging us on, so I hopped up and followed her toward the nearby metro station.

Now I freely admit it, Dear Readers. I was not paying attention because I knew Charlotte was taking care of everything. I was actually thinking, twisted as it was, that the stinking-rich American broad in Parisian couture might be a PERFECT character for my novel. What a great way to start the book! This creature is toodling around Paris in her million-dollar French garb, and she thinks she's All That. But what the reader instantly sees, because I so deftly and subtly render it so, is that this woman doesn't represent Paris at all. That she isn't the real thing. That she's more like Lindy Sloane trying to perform Shakespeare. Totally out of place, totally out of her league. And she has no idea. But WE know.

I was on a ROLL! *This* was why I was in Paris! To experience an Unprecedented Stream of Creative Consciousness! I started trying to think up whom the tacky character could encounter, you know, to display in *crude* and *excruciating* ways how clueless she really was. I was getting it! Material for my Great Parisian Novel! So you know, I could hardly be expected to pay a great deal of attention to my current surroundings. I just had to follow Charlotte, as usual. She knew where we needed to go. She knew what train to take. She knew how to get a ticket and what to do with it.

Charlotte was descending some kind of staircase, and I hurried after her, thinking furiously. When I stopped behind her at some kind of booth, I started imagining what the character's voice would sound like. What kind of accent she had. And to do that, I had to tune out the sounds of my friends altogether. Well, almost altogether. As I followed them through a gate and toward the track, I was dimly aware that Charlotte was speaking. The Long Island accent worked perfectly for the character, I decided. I tried out her voice in my head. Somewhere in the back of my mind I was aware of Charlotte's voice too, muffled by the sound of a train arriving. A crowd of people pressed forward, and so did I. I could still hear my character's Texan twang mingling with Charlotte shouting something as I stepped onto the train. It was only when the doors closed and Charlotte's voice was suddenly much more muffled that I realized what she'd been saying. Parts of what she'd been saying. Words like *Wrong. Direction. Train. Guys. Other. Side.*

I was on the Wrong Train. I was on the Wrong Train going in the Wrong Direction, and the last thing I saw was Charlotte's startled face through the window, mouthing something like "Lily You Are on the Wrong Train."

Then the train rumbled on through the tunnel, with me unfortunately and unhappily on it. The worst fears of Phyllis Blennerhasset and Madame Chavotte had come to pass.

I, Lily Blennerhasset, had become Separated from the Group.

Six

If any of the French people on the train noticed my horror-stricken expression, or heard my heart pounding like a jackhammer, or saw my mouth frozen open in an *O* of Despair, they didn't say anything. I was completely paralyzed, probably complicating the situation since the first few times the train stopped, I was too afraid to get off. I had this idea that if I just stayed on long enough, the train would eventually loop back to the place where I'd gotten on. This might have been a sound theory, but with a little investigative thought I realized I had NO idea of the name of the stop where I'd gotten on. Which led me to the even more sickening thought that I wasn't precisely sure where the VEI was either. The street had a person's name, like the Rue Will Ferrell or something, but my memory wouldn't be more specific.

Dear Readers, you simply cannot imagine the State of Terror which I was in. I had committed the Cardinal Infraction: In spite of REPEATED warnings from MULTIPLE sources, I had become Separated from the Group. I did not know the address where I was staying. I did not know where I had just been. I did not have a Working Conversational Understanding of French, except when it involved vocabulary words that I had for some arbitrary reason retained in my memory. I did not even know where the train I had boarded was going.

I was all kinds of Lost.

Only now did I realize why certain authority figures had been so insistent that I NOT become Separated from the Group. Because apparently there was no way that I was ever, EVER going to find my way back again. I didn't even know where back was! Separation from the Group apparently involved THE END OF MY ENTIRE LIFE AS I HAD KNOWN IT. I was going to become an expatriate bag lady, walking the cobblestone streets year after year, looking for my Group.

All right. I had to at least try to do SOMETHING before giving up and acknowledging that I was Forever Lost, doomed to wander the streets, muttering about Lindy Sloane's latest hair color. Maybe someone on the train spoke English. But even in English, what would I ask? Nobody on this train could tell me in any language how to get back to my Group, because none of them knew who my Group was. At least if I could remember the name of the station where I'd just been, I'd be slightly better off than I was now, hurtling into the Parisian unknown. Could I remember the street names? Could I remember ANYTHING?

Then it hit me. Before Bonnie's past life memories took over, we had been heading for Victor Hugo's house. VICTOR HUGO WOULD SAVE ME! Who better to save a writer than another writer? If I could get back to the stop nearest Hugo's house, I ought to be back at the metro stop where I'd gotten on the Wrong Train. Then I could find the RIGHT train, the one going toward the Louvre. I'd have to wing it after that, but surely I could wing? Somebody at the Victor Hugo station would speak English and have maps and directions. Because I HAD to be at the Louvre this afternoon! Madame Chavotte didn't know that I had become Separated from the Group. And she mustn't know! She wouldn't know! Unless I did not manage to get to the Louvre in time for the tour. If I failed to do that, then she would know. And what had she said? There would be no more TREEPS! There would be NUSSING!

Madame Chavotte must at all costs NEVER know I had become Separated from the Group! I took a deep breath and summoned up the courage to ask exactly one person, in English, the name of the metro stop closest to the house of Victor Hugo. I was given a very pinched look, like I was wearing an overripe slab of goat cheese for a hat, and the curt dismissal *"Je ne parle que français."* Literally, "I not speak but French." That was vocabulary that my brain HAD retained. The situation was Officially Desperate. I became utterly consumed with the Enormity of my Mistake.

So this is why the train passed a few more stops (three? five? seven?) before it occurred to me, like a rat on a sinking ship, to get off. Which I did. And though I'm aware I had not to this point exactly displayed Keen Intelligence or even Common Sense, I did have the presence of mind to find my way to the train going in the opposite direction and get on that one. I even had a Small Burst of Brain in which I calculated that I should stay on this train slightly longer than I'd been on the anti-Louvre train, since Charlotte clearly intended us to travel in that direction for a few stops. I tried to gain some confidence from my Small Burst of Brain, but the truth is when I finally decided it was time to get off the anti-anti-Louvre train, I was more lost than a duck in the stock market.

After I walked up to the street, cars whizzed by and well-dressed *Parisiennes* strode smartly past on their high heels. That's when I really began to feel alone. Like Stanley staggering through the forest of the Congo in search of Dr. Livingstone. Like Dian Fossey hacking her way through the mountain foliage in search of African gorillas. Like Luke Skywalker facing those very bad guys in plastic armor. Seriously.

So you can imagine the great wave of relief that swept over me when, after a block or two of aimless rambling, I came upon something that I RECOGNIZED! There it was, looming ahead of me, a massive monument around which the entire city seemed to be circling. It was a giant stone arch, covered with carvings, that I had seen and even visited more than once before. There was only one problem. The monument I recognized was the Washington Square Arch. Which meant that I was on Fifth Avenue. In New York City. On the eastern coast of the United States of America.

This left me with several possibilities:

1. I had been more distracted than previously realized and had traveled three thousand miles beneath the Atlantic Ocean before getting off the train.
2. I was seeing a giant inflatable Washington Square Arch erected by Parisians bent on confusing and confounding visiting New Yorkers.
3. A Rare Astronomical Anomaly caused by a Bizarre Planetary Alignment was causing rays

from the sun to bounce off the Washington Square Arch and beam the image to Paris, creating a Transatlantic Optical Illusion.
4. There was a similar arch in Paris whose existence I had not been aware of.

Oh, why, WHY was it always at the Diabolically Darkest Moments of My Life that I had occasion to realize how RIGHT Charlotte had been about something? I was wrong to have slacked off the way I had. The only research I had done on Paris was to flip through my old Madeline books. The guidebook my mother had given me was still packed away with other items I deemed unnecessary, like SPF 80 sunblock. Charlotte appeared to know the location of every landmark within a fifty-mile radius of the city. Even Bonnie was able to find a home she had not lived in for four centuries without any difficulty. But I knew nothing of the landscape of Paris because I hadn't thought it was necessary for me, personally, to prepare. As Janet might say, I was *la disgrâce*.

To make matters worse, I stole a quick glance at my watch and discovered that it was fifteen minutes before one. I was supposed to be at ze glesspairmeed, despite the fact that I did not know what ze glesspairmeed was, in fifteen minutes or Madame Chavotte would know that I had become Separated from the Group. And then everyone would be punished, and no Mulgrew eighth-almost-ninth graders would EVER be privileged to travel overseas again. All. Because. Of. Me.

Crapstick.

I had to start moving. I had to get myself in the direction of the Louvre and worry about ze glesspairmeed when I got there.

"Louvre?" I asked a random passerby. I got the goat-cheese–hat look again. Perhaps I should pick someone who was not so sharply dressed. I needed to go for someone older. Everyone knows that the Elderly Are Kind.

"Louvre?" I asked a kindly-looking elderly gentleman. I was immensely gratified when he stopped in front of me, giving me his complete attention.

"Pardon?" he asked.

"I'm trying to get to the Louvre?" I said, making a question out of that sad fact. In addition, I'm sure I wasn't saying the name correctly. Pronouncing it "the Loover" sounded wrong somehow. "The museum?" I mimed painting a picture.

Apparently, NONE of the French words I needed to communicate with this man had been retained in my brain. Instead, my brain suddenly fired strange synapses filled with French words I COULD recall, but that had NO bearing on my present situation. *Cadeau* means gift. *La mer* means the sea. *Chewing-gum* means chewing gum.

And since I did not want or need to request a gift of chewing gum from the sea, I was obviously doomed.

My mother had insisted that most Parisians spoke English, but she'd also told me that most Parisians left Paris in August, leaving me with a city full of visitors who had probably just gotten off the bus from that French-Place-in-the-Distant-Mountainsville and spoke no English.

I took a final stab.

"Mona Lisa?" I asked, making another little painting gesture in the air.

"Ah, bien, le Louvre!" said the man, breaking into a smile.

Loo-vruh. Aha!

I nodded so vigorously, it's amazing my head didn't fly off and roll all the way back to the monument that was NOT the Washington Square Arch.

"Tu es perdu, ma petite poulette?"

I'm not sure, but I think the Kindly Elderly Gentleman had just addressed me as "my little chicken." I know that because the last week of French class we read a picture book about a brave little chicken, and it was called *La Poulette Courageuse*, and I had made fun of it, asking who in the world would ever benefit from reading such a ridiculous piece of writing. The answer, apparently, was me.

"Mais tu parles un peu français, non?" he continued.

I, Lily Blennerhassett, the Little Chicken, nodded. Because I was better at understanding French than speaking it. The sentence meant "But you speak a little French, no?" And you see, when I NODDED, my intention was to be agreeing with the NO part. I speak a little French NO. I NO speak NO French NO. Yes, I am supposed to speak French and I have spoken it before and just yesterday I correctly translated the meaning of (but not the location of) *deuxième étage*, and I can ask for a gift of chewing gum from the sea, but for the moment let's all just agree, Dear Readers, that I speak French NO. Wherever you put the NO word in English, it's right there. No. NO!! And it should be PAINFULLY OBVIOUS that I NO spoke a little French because I had addressed the man in English from the start.

It was too late, though. The man started chattering away in French, the merry smile never leaving his face, as he jabbed in the air, indicating lefts and rights and this ways and that ways. And I, the Little Chicken, nodded and smiled and made the "ah, yes, I understand completely" face until he finally stopped and in his Kindly Elderly Manner he waved me along.

At least I had gotten the general direction. I was on a main street—it was wide and busy and full of shops and restaurants (like Fifth Avenue, where I now recognized I was NOT)—so it obviously went somewhere important and the Kindly Elderly Man had clearly indicated his Little Chicken was to proceed down it.

Progress.

I looked at my watch. It was eight minutes before one.

I began to jog. Though I interviewed no witnesses, I feel certain that the sight of a little American chicken jogging down the street, red-faced and wheezing, was not going to improve any international reputations.

I jogged as long as I could. Then I stopped and clutched my leg in alarm, letting out a little shriek that signaled approaching doom. I had injured myself. Possibly gravely. Possibly fatally. I felt no pain, but my entire right leg was shuddering. It was convulsing in agony. I grabbed my thigh muscle and squeezed.

There was something in my pocket. I reached in frantically and pulled the thing out. It was small and dark and vibrating, and it looked like a phaser from *Star Trek*. But before I had the chance to scream and hurl it into the street, I realized what it was. It was the cell phone that my mother had given me. And I remembered that my father, Esteemed Law Abider Lenny Blennerhassett, who is Diametrically Opposed to All Cell Phones for Any Reason but Grudgingly Accepts Their Role in Personal Safety, had painstakingly followed the instruction booklet and programmed my phone to vibrate, not ring, so as not to violate the Personal Listening Space of other people.

Someone was calling me. I had no idea who it could be, and I didn't care to guess. Someone was reaching out to touch me, at a moment when I'd never felt more alone.

I jabbed the phone against my ear and barked, "Hello?"

The phone kept vibrating.

Why, oh, WHY, had I not learned how to operate this machine?

I stared at the phone. Buttons. Many buttons. One of them was green. Green! The international signal for GO! I pushed it and frantically put the phone to my ear again.

"HELLO?" I shrieked.

No one was there. What kind of cruel trick was this? I stared at the phone again. Maybe I'd hit the wrong button.

Wait a minute. There was something written on my little display screen.

where r u?

What kind of question was that? It was patently obvious that I was lost, and now my PHONE wanted to know where I was?

"I'm lost, stupid!" I yelled at the phone. Nothing happened.

Wait.

WAIT!

I had another Small Burst of Brain. My phone wasn't talking to me. It was typing to me!

Maybe I was supposed to type back.

what?

The little cursor blinked on and off. As an afterthought, I hit the green button, and my words disappeared.

where r u?

All sorts of witty responses occurred to me. But I was alone and lost in Paris, and my phone was trying to make friends with me. It might pay to be concise.

lost. where r u?

Then I thought about it, and added:

who r u?

I waited. And waited. Until:

Lewis @ the Louvre

"LEWIS?!" I shouted at the phone. "What do you mean, Lewis? How can you be Lewis?"

The cursor blinked at me, just as confused. A few people shot the cheese look in my direction and hurried by.

how why help

I typed rapidly. Though it goes against every fiber in my

being to write sentence fragments and use convenience spellings like "u," I was one desperate Little Chicken, and I didn't want Lewis to go away.

For a minute no message came back, and I began to panic. But then suddenly the screen filled with words.

> ok. told mdme c just saw u. thinks u r in bathrm.

This seemed to require a response:

> ok and?

Lewis shot back:

> gt hr as sn as psble. msg me whn u r here. gtta go 4 now.

Gotta go for now?

"NO!" I yelled at the phone. "You have to tell me where HERE is!"

Then I typed it. But Lewis was gone. Apparently he was buying me some time. I had to get to the Louvre, fast.

Jogging was simply out of the question. I settled for an ants-in-the-pants kind of speed walk. Have you ever tried to rush somewhere when you don't know where you're going? I'm sure it looks all kinds of stupid.

I was going to have to ask someone else for directions, and I just didn't have time to mess around with the French and be called the diminutive form of another barnyard animal. I needed to find a Tourist. At this point, even a Simple Tourist would do.

I looked down the street before crossing it, and there they were, gleaming golden and familiar in the sunlight like a beacon of hope in an ocean of despair. The Icon of Recognizability. The Object of Every Lost Soul's Hopes and Dreams.

The Golden Arches.

The Blennerhassetts are not, as a rule, a McDonald's family. We go only once a year, as an elaborate staged "accident," on the way to our lake house when my dad pretends to get lost. But right now it looked like home. I trotted toward it with desperation.

There was a guy standing outside the door, talking to a girl in a large floppy hat and enormous sunglasses. I did a classic double take, unable to believe my eyes. The sad slouch and hands thrust deep in pockets were unmistakable. It was the Mysterious Tim, not looking sick to his stomach at all. The Mysterious Tim, big as life right there outside Mickey Dees, *chez* Paris. Why or how he had got there was the least of my concerns. Perhaps no one had ever heard him speak, but the chances were excellent that he could, and that when he did, it would be in ENGLISH!

I took off in a sprint toward him.

"TIM!" I bellowed. He turned and looked at me right away. When he saw me, his jaw dropped, and he took a step backward. I skidded to a stop inches before knocking him down.

"Tim, thank GOD!" I yelled. "I'm lost and I'm supposed to be at the Louvre right now and I don't know how to get there and Lewis is covering for me but Madame Chavotte is going to figure it out when I don't come back from the bathroom and everyone will be expelled because of me and I've got to get there fast but I have no idea how far it is and if I should get back on the train or try to get a cab which I don't even know how to DO in French and you've GOT to help me!"

I only stopped because I needed to breathe. Between heaving gasps, I heard the girl say something, possibly in Italian. Did NO ONE in this town speak English?

"Of course she's not paparazzi," Tim said to her. "She's a girl from my class."

Paparazzi?

In spite of my plight, I turned to check the girl out. You know. For my Mental Pool. And I beheld the face of the very last person I ever expected to see on This Planet or Any Other.

Lindy Sloane.

Seven

It was like one of those standoffs in an old western movie. Slack-jawed, I stared at Lindy. She stared back at me, face dwarfed behind the giant, buglike glasses. The two of us just stood there, neither taking her eyes off the other. If Clint Eastwood were here, he'd put two fingers on his holster and say, "Draaaaaaaaaaaaaaaw."

But Clint Eastwood was not here.

"Why are you staring at me?" asked Lindy Sloane.

Why was I staring at her? Let's review the top five reasons:

1. She was on the cover of every magazine except *The Economist* that had been published in the last six months.

2. Already this year she had made two movies, launched her own pajama design line, released a signature collection of edible hair products, been given the key to Tulsa, Oklahoma, appeared on her own MTV reality show to document the making of her new CD, endorsed a series of experimental hybrid SUV convertibles, written a children's book, guest hosted *American Idol*, been engaged to and subsequently dumped the lead singer of Savage Karma, and caused a near riot in the Mall of America.

3. She was worshiped and revered by a bizarre group of teenagers calling themselves the Sloane Rangers, who spent hours on the Internet discussing her every move. They copied her clothes, hair, and mannerisms, and had even been known to paint freckles on their shoulders in the same places Lindy Sloane had freckles.

4. She was close personal friends with Houston Ramada, celebutante and internationally photographed bad girl.

5. I had absolutely nothing like her in my Mental Pool.

Okay. That was reason enough.

"Why are you staring at me?" Lindy Sloane repeated impatiently.

"Phletamgah."

Sorry, but that's what came out of my mouth. Strangely, Lindy gave a small nod, as if I'd inadvertently stumbled upon the correct password.

"What are you doing here?" asked Tim.

I looked at him in astonishment. Hearing the Mysterious Tim speaking in regular sentences was going to take some getting used to. It didn't feel right. I kept expecting bats to fly out of his mouth, or something.

"What are YOU doing here?" I asked him. "I thought you had to stay behind at the VEI because you were sick."

"I asked you first," Tim said.

Ah. Shrewd.

I needed to forget for the moment that I was standing outside McDonald's *chez* Paris with Lindy Sloane and provide Tim with some information so I could get some out of him.

"I got on the Wrong Train," I said. "Before I realized what was happening, I was being whisked away, and Bonnie and Charlotte and Janet were still standing on the platform. Now I'm trying meet them at the Louvre before Madame Chavotte realizes I'm missing. Because if she finds out I got Separated from the Group, everybody's going to get in big trouble. But I have no idea how to get there. Your turn."

Tim kind of glowered at me silently.

"Look, Tim, I've already seen you here, so I know you're playing hooky. If you get caught, we all get in trouble. I'm not going to tell on you, and I'm sure you have no intention of telling on me. But I told you my story."

"Yeah, all right," he said. "I faked being sick."

There was a long pause.

"And you are here because?" I prompted.

Tim gave a deep sigh and rubbed the top of his head. "Because I needed to see my sister."

I looked around. "Did you find her?"

Tim looked at me like he'd just noticed the word *stupid* written across my forehead.

"This IS my sister," he said, gesturing toward Lindy Sloane, who was applying lip gloss with a tube that appeared to have her picture on it.

Wait.

WHAT?

It was bizarre, ridiculous, and highly improbable. Nobody could keep a secret like THAT. But even as I was starting to roll my eyes, I took a closer look at Tim. And then I saw it. If you dyed Lindy's hair brown, removed the makeup, made her eat a few sandwiches, stuck her in a dark T-shirt, and removed some freckles . . . well, they weren't exactly twins, but I could see the family resemblance.

"But that's—that's—"

"Lindy Sloane," said Lindy Sloane. "Duh."

"How? Why? How?" I demanded. "Tim, this is simply unreal!"

"Slick, T," Lindy said. "You're going to have to change schools again." She pulled off her big hat, shook her newly blond curls dramatically, and plopped the hat back onto her head. I tried not to look, but this was the closest I'd ever been to Hollywood glamour, and I didn't want to miss anything.

"Change schools?" I asked.

Tim sighed.

"Last year, right after Lindy hit it big, some kids at my old school figured out she was my sister. I'd only been there a year."

"I was eighteen. I already had my own condo in L.A.," Lindy said, making a pouty, camera-friendly face.

"And the word got out, and I was, like, mobbed," Tim continued.

"Sloane Rangers?" I asked, using a concerned look favored by famous television reporters.

"Yeah, they were the worst. Suddenly everyone wanted to be my best friend. Everyone followed me around. All these girls called me. They stopped by unannounced. It was all, like, Lindy this and Lindy that. These people didn't even have tact, man. They didn't even try to pretend they weren't using me to get to Lindy."

"Until—" Lindy interjected, possibly because it was not her nature to stray from center stage for too long.

"Until the straw that broke the camel's back," Tim said. "One day these three girls stopped by, you know, like they're interested in me. And one of them sneaks upstairs into the bathroom and opens the linen closet, and she steals this old retainer of Lindy's that's still in there with her name printed on the case. And I found out about it three days later when the thing comes up for auction on eBay! Lindy Sloane's retainer, orthodontist verified."

Ouch.

"Starting bid was seventy-five dollars," Lindy said. "It sold for two hundred and twenty."

"Same thing happened at sailing camp that summer," Tim continued. "This is all the way up in Maine, okay, so I figured nobody knew who I was. But somehow the word got out, and the next thing I know, somebody rips off two letters from my mother—my *mother*! And they set up this little booth and charged a buck a pop for kids to see the actual handwriting of Lindy Sloane's mom. A buck fifty if you wanted to hold the letter yourself."

"Over one hundred customers, and more turned away," Lindy added.

"So . . . your last name is *Sloane*?" I asked Tim.

"No, and neither is hers," Tim said. "Her real name is

 94

Linda Mildred Dorfman."

"Shut up, worm!" Lindy shouted, swatting Tim on the arm with her enormous Balenciaga purse. For the first time they actually acted like siblings. But only for a minute. Then Lindy regained her star composure, whipped off her gigantic sunglasses, and stared at me with intense, heavily made-up eyes.

"Well, you know, I don't have to tell anyone," I said.

Wait. I didn't? What was I saying?

"Yeah, right," said Tim.

"Is this why you're so . . . I mean, you never, *ever* talk to anybody. It's like this big mystery at school. That you never, you know, *speak*."

"Talking leads to conversations, which lead to questions, which lead to people figuring out who my sister is, which leads to the ruination of my life," said Tim. "It's better just not to know anyone at all."

Gee, he was actually opening up a little.

"I keep telling you to move to L.A. with me and Mom. Go to Beverly Hills High. Everybody there is related to somebody famous."

"I detest Los Angeles," Tim said.

Yeah. Me too.

"Lindy e-mailed me that she was taking a few days off from filming and coming incognito to Paris. I figured we could meet up here, and nobody would be the wiser. And

I'm not even standing next to her ten minutes when, of course, some girl from school runs over."

It took me a moment to realize that some girl from school referred to me.

"But I won't tell anybody," I insisted.

I'm not sure I actually believed that while the words were coming out of my mouth. I mean, this was LINDY SLOANE. Imagine the look on Charlotte's face . . . on EVERYBODY'S face, when I told this story! And Tim, the Mysterious Tim, turning out to be Lindy's little brother! It was the SCOOP OF THE DECADE. I would be mobbed back at Mulgrew; everybody would want to hear the details from my lips. And how brilliantly I would tell the story! How tantalizing its unfolding! I would hold court in the cafeteria, my audience eager and breathless as I related each—

And then I realized something. I *couldn't* tell anybody. Not even Charlotte. Not even Jake. This was Tim's secret, not mine. And if I blabbed it all over Mulgrew Middle School, I would certainly increase my social standing and become Enormously Sought After and Astoundingly Popular, but Tim would have to leave school. At least that's what he would feel he needed to do. By telling the story, I would totally mess up Tim's life. And then I would be no better than the girl who'd stolen Lindy's retainer and sold it on eBay. I would be no better than

Princess Diana's butler, who accepted her friendship and confidences, then blabbed about it in a book after she died. If I told everybody who Tim really was, I would be nothing but a Tell-All Girl.

No. I couldn't do that. It might practically *kill* me, but the only place this information was going was into my Mental Pool, where of course all names are changed to protect the innocent.

"Why should I believe you?" Tim asked. "I don't even know you."

"But you do know me now, Tim. I'm Lily Blenner-hassett. I'm a Writer."

"I wrote a book," said Lindy, examining her manicure. "It was easy. Sold two hundred thousand copies the first week."

For one very brief moment I entertained the idea of ripping Lindy Sloane's hat and glasses off, then running into McDonald's and revealing her immediate location to every tourist I could find. Because there is nothing, and I do mean NOTHING, more irritating to me than a celebrity who decides to write a book and claims it's "easy." Houston Ramada had "written a book" too: a thinly veiled novel following her international celebu-tante adventures. About a month after it came out, the actual writer of the book came forward. She said she'd never even met Houston Ramada. She'd been hired by

Ramada's publicist, written the whole thing herself, and e-mailed it to the publisher. Nobody cared, and the book stayed on the bestseller list for ages.

But I digress.

"You'll just have to wait and see, Tim. I'm not going to tell. This information is in the Vault."

Tim looked a little hopeful, but not too hopeful. It was the look of guarded optimism that can come only from a guy whose sister's orthodontics were once purloined for profit.

"People, we need to MOVE," Lindy barked suddenly. "I've probably already been spotted. *Star* magazine has photographers that follow me on EVERY CONTINENT."

I wanted to ask Lindy to name all the continents, just for fun, but I restrained myself—because it seemed mean-spirited, if not also hysterically funny. Anyway, the mention of needing to move jolted me back to the Reality of My Plight. I looked at my watch. It was one fifteen.

"Oh my God! I've got to get to the Louvre! Tim, do you have any idea where it is?"

"Not really," he replied. "Sorry. I didn't think I was going to need to know."

"I know where the Louvre is," said Lindy, in the same tone that she'd used to tell me she'd written a book.

I swallowed.

"Really? Honestly?" I asked. "Like, not just where it is,

 98

but where it is in relation to here? And where here is? And how to get there?"

Lindy sighed and adjusted the oh-so-wide belt on her oh-so-low-riding jeans.

"Darling, I know Paris like the back of my hand," she said. "And I did a photo shoot at the Louvre last month for Milk of Human Kindness International."

"Really?" I asked.

Lindy looked bored.

"It's down the Champs-Elysées and over to the Rue de Rivoli. Past the Jardin des Tuileries."

It did not escape my notice that Lindy Sloane had a perfect French accent.

"Well, how long will it take me to walk there?"

Lindy bestowed upon me a look of sheer astonishment.

"Walk?" she asked. She appeared to consider the word, then repeated it again with the same level of bewilderment. *"Walk?"*

"Well, uh . . . what do you suggest?"

Lindy turned and made a grand gesture toward the curb with her hand, like Moses parting the Red Sea. And then I saw it. How could I not have seen it before? It looked like an ocean liner with tinted windows docked in a marina full of rowboats.

"Get in," said Lindy.

There may have been all sorts of reasons, environmental and otherwise, why I should not get into Lindy Sloane's stretch limo, but I didn't produce any of them. Time was of the essence, and who was I to look a gift celebrity in the mouth?

As we approached, a uniformed driver magically appeared and opened the back door. It didn't so much feel like getting into a car as it felt like going into someone's living room. There was a television, a fridge, a phone, a bar. Lindy Sloane's limousine could have provided ground support to a small army for several days.

"I so utterly and completely appreciate this," I said to Tim as he climbed in next to me. "You're a good guy."

He shrugged, but I couldn't help thinking he looked a little . . . pleased.

Lindy slid expertly into the seat across from me. This was a person who'd had plenty of practice getting into limousines. Out of the sunlight, her face was almost entirely shadowed by her sunglasses. When the driver got behind the wheel, Lindy spoke.

"Jean-Michel, nous avons besoin d'aller au Musée du Louvre tout de suite, s'il te plaît. La demoiselle ici est bien en retard."

My goodness! While I was still relatively certain Lindy could not correctly name all the continents, I have to admit I was impressed by her French.

The limousine moved surprising fast through the traffic, in a *Titanic* sort of way.

"What are you going to do when you get there?" Tim asked. "I mean, isn't the Louvre supposed to be huge?"

"I don't know," I said. "I'm making this up as I go. Everybody was supposed to meet at this place called ze glesspairmeed. Do you have any idea what that is?"

"*Glace* means 'ice cream,'" stated Lindy.

"*Père* means 'father,'" added Tim.

"So you think it's an ice-cream stand?" I asked eagerly. "Called Father something?"

Tim pulled a small dictionary out of a little pocket by his door.

"Don't leave home without it," he said, flipping through the pages. "What's the last part? *Meed?* I don't see . . . there's a *midinette.*"

"What's it mean?" I asked.

"Uh . . . silly young townie."

"Father's Silly Young Townie Ice-Cream Stand?" I asked.

"It's catchy," said Lindy.

"Keep looking," I said to Tim.

"The only other thing that sounds close is *midi*. It means noon."

"Father's Noon Ice-Cream Stand," I said thoughtfully. "I don't know. It could be a French thing."

"I've never heard of it," Lindy said. At this point I was

willing to accept her opinion as expert.

"Well, do you have any ideas? Do you remember any ice-cream stands from your photo shoot?"

Lindy wrinkled her nose. "We had an on-set buffet," she said. "You don't really think I'd go to some ice-cream stand with all of the Other People, do you?"

As one of the Other People, I felt mildly offended. But this was not a good time to launch a grass-roots Other People movement.

"I just thought you might have noticed something," I responded diplomatically.

"I have people whose job is to notice things FOR me," Lindy said. "I have a STAFF. Hair guy, makeup guy, Pilates guy, nutrition guy, color consultant guy, life coach guy. You know."

Uh-huh. Well, I had Charlotte. So I could kind of relate.

"Voilà, nous sommes arrivés au Louvre," the driver was saying.

I perked up at the sound of the word *Louvre*. I looked out the window. This must be the place. Victory! Yay!

Jean-Michel hopped out of the car and opened the back door. I started to slide out, then paused.

"Listen, I seriously want to thank you. Both of you. You're, like, saving my life here."

"Whatever." Lindy shrugged. She pulled out her cell

phone and began to fuss with it.

But Tim kind of smiled a little, which seemed as dramatic a change as Helen Keller at the pump spelling out w-a-t-e-r for the first time. Progress.

"What are you going to do now?" he asked.

"I'm not sure," I replied. "Once I'm inside the museum, at least I'm there. It may take a while to find everybody, but we'll be in the same building."

Tim nodded thoughtfully.

"What about you?" I asked.

Lindy had called someone on her cell and was chattering away about a stylist whom a friend had fired. She sounded outraged and bored at the same time.

"We'll drive around, maybe go over to the Tuileries or Versailles or something. Except for you, nobody's recognized her yet. Maybe we'll get lucky and stay anonymous."

"Definitely," I told him. Secretly, I have to say the chances of Lindy Sloane's remaining incognito for long, even in her monster hat and bug glasses, were slimmer than she was. And that's saying something.

"I'll be back at the VEI before you guys," he said.

"Don't worry about it if you're late," I said. "I've got your back."

Then I made this ridiculous little "key locking the lips" motion. I don't know what I was thinking.

But Tim seemed pleased.

"Later," he said.

"Later," I replied.

I admit, Dear Readers, I snuck a final peek at Lindy Sloane before stepping back so that Jean-Michel could close the limousine door. It was just as well that I didn't plan on telling anybody. I can't think of a person in the world who would believe it.

I waved a cheery good-bye to the sleek whale of an automobile. It was impossible to tell through the tinted windows if anyone waved back.

Then I turned to have a look at the Louvre and evaluate my next move.

Crapstick.

I've been to large museums before. But this building looked like its own CITY. It seemed to stretch elegantly and endlessly in every direction. I was willing to bet the entire population of Greenland could be inside that building AT THIS VERY MOMENT, and there would still be plenty of elbow room. How did a person even get INSIDE this place? There were crowds of people everywhere. But in the midst of the frenzy of activity, I noticed a stream of bodies going in and out through an archway. Quickly, I followed them.

The courtyard seemed roughly the size of Rhode Island. To my left I could see another huge arch monument. They seemed to be following me. And to my right was the heart of the U-shaped palace that was the Louvre. There might be an admission door over there somewhere. Who could see anything with that huge glass pyramid smack in the center of things?

Glass pyramid.

Glesspairmeed.

EUREKA!

Eight

There was an entrance right in the glass pyramid, which led to an escalator going down to a gleaming marble-floored reception area. Now, I say "reception area," but it looked like a very streamlined version of the engine room on the starship *Enterprise*. Overhead, the glass pyramid soared into the sky. I pitied the Louvre's Official Window Washer.

I had stumbled upon a mecca of English speakers. Even women in saris and men in elaborate headdresses were speaking English. At the admissions desk I didn't bother explaining my situation. The nice lady in the trim blue suit who spoke perfect English certainly wouldn't know where Madame Chavotte and her students had gone. I paid for a student ticket, took a few authoritative steps down a hallway, then stopped.

How was I going to locate my group in a four-story building of this magnitude? Being lost in the Louvre might be just as hopeless as being lost in Paris, and statistically I was unlikely to run into another celebrity willing to direct me where I needed to go.

Then I remembered Lewis. He'd said to text message him when I got to the museum. Sadly, he hadn't told me HOW to do that. Or maybe he had, and I wasn't paying attention. I pulled out my phone and stared at it. I pushed a button. Nothing happened. I pushed another button. Nothing happened. I pushed a bunch of buttons in succession. All at once the phone produced a high-pitched single-tone version of Mozart's *Eine Kleine Nachtmusik*. I let out a little yell, shook the phone and smacked it, then tried sticking it under my arm to muffle the sound. People began staring at the Little Chicken with Mozart coming out of her armpit, so I started pushing buttons again. Miraculously the music stopped. What a nightmare!

I decided to push one last button. I picked one on the side of the phone. A menu flashed onto the screen. Now we were getting somewhere! With things looking more computerlike and less phonelike, I became more confident. Even the superpowers of Lenny Blennerhassett had not prevented me from getting a moderate amount of experience using e-mail. I found my way through "text message" to "address book," and YAY! Lewis had indeed entered his address there.

After a few wrong turns, I finally sent Lewis a message:

im here

The response came back almost immediately.

good—cant cvr mch lngr—hrry up flr 2.

Eureka! I made a dash for the elevator, holding the phone out in front of me like it was a homing device. As I got into the elevator, my hand froze over the buttons. Was floor two the second floor or the *deuxième étage* that made it the third floor? But I had come in a floor *below* street level. So maybe in this building the *deuxième étage* was the second floor because the ground floor was the first floor and the subterranean level the ground floor?

I hit "2" and let the elevator decide what it meant. When the door opened, I got off and text messaged Lewis:

b mr spcfc. whr r u?

A lady with a baby stroller almost ran me down as I waited for his reply.

paintings

Well, thank you very much. That was Extremely Helpful. I'm in the world's largest collection of artwork, and Lewis tells me to meet him BY THE PAINTINGS.

details

I made a face at the screen when I hit "send," just to reinforce my feelings of exasperation.

fat guard w teeny mstche. grp of abt 100 german kids. ldy w triplets in stroller.

I looked around frantically in every direction, but I didn't see any of those things. Well, not exactly. I saw a guard with a teeny mustache, but he was thin. I saw a group of about a hundred kids, but they looked Japanese. I saw two ladies with strollers, but both had sets of twins. Paintings I saw. Paintings EVERYWHERE. Millions upon millions of them.

Crapstick.

I would have to search systematically, wing by wing. That should only take, according to what I could glean from the map the admissions lady gave me, about three hours. Per floor. I had barely started down the Hall of

Painted Grim Guys in Big Hats and Dark Colors when my phone wiggled. (I preferred to think of it as wiggling; vibrating sounded too dental.)

gng to escltr

What? They were switching floors? Now I'd have to switch floors too, assuming I was on the right floor to start with. At this point everything felt like the dumb-*ième étage* to me. I shot off a message:

wht drctn?

And after a moment, I got back:

down 1

I went back in the direction I'd come, once again through the Hall of Painted Grim Guys in Big Hats and Dark Colors. There was a little group of plump blond women posing for a picture, the escalator beyond them. I dashed through the shot just as the photographer was exhorting them to "say cheese." I have no doubt I will make a notable addition to someone's vacation photo album.

As I sprinted out onto the first floor, my phone wiggled again.

baby cryng by wndow

I stopped and listened. I seemed to hear crying babies from every direction.

Another wiggle from the phone.

monalisa!!!

International jackpot! I scuttled over to the closest security guard.

"Hi there . . . um . . . English?"

"What are you looking for?" he said in slightly accented English, eyes half closed like I'd caught him napping.

"Mona L—"

He cut me off.

"Down that hall, right, fourth hallway on the left, look for the crowd."

"Thank you," I said. He seemed to have fallen back asleep. I guess an American asking directions to the *Mona Lisa* wasn't very unusual or interesting. He probably stood there all day telling people where the *Mona Lisa* was. I hoped, for his sake, a tiny but ultimately failed armed robbery might happen after I'd left—just a little something for him to talk about with his buddies after work.

I shot down the hallway like a speed skater, bobbing

around and between people. When I got to the fourth hallway on the left, I saw the crowd right away. If I'd been anywhere else, I would have assumed there'd been some kind of accident. But I could see very well what the crowd was staring at. Hanging by itself on the wall, protected by velvet ropes preventing anyone from approaching too closely, was the *Mona Lisa*. The painting looked a lot smaller than I'd expected. Like maybe the size of one of those posters of a kitten hanging off a branch that say, "Hang on, it's almost Friday!" When something is a Universally Recognized Artistic Icon of Epic Proportions, you expect it to be at least the size of a station wagon. Still, I needed to capture the moment for my Mental Pool, which is what I was doing when I heard an unmistakable voice above the crowd.

"She is *magnifique, n'est-ce pas?* She is *formidable!*"

I sidled over, all casual.

"She's not even French, Janet. She's Italian."

Janet whirled to face me.

"Where have you been?" she demanded. "Lewis keeps saying he just saw you, but I haven't laid eyes on you since we got separated at *le métro*."

"Where else would I be? I've been right here," I said.

Janet regarded me suspiciously. I gave a little carefree laugh.

"What, you don't believe me?" I asked. "You need, like,

 112

proof? We rendezvoused at the glass pyramid. Upstairs, where that big security guard with the tiny mustache was, I almost fell over a stroller pushing triplets. Right by that big group of German kids. And you . . . you've been speaking in French since the moment we got here!"

Janet looked genuinely puzzled to be confronted by these truths, so I took the opportunity to flounce away. I flounced right into Charlotte. My soaring spirits were immediately dampened by the severely outraged look on Charlotte's face. She glanced around to make sure no one was listening, then tugged me by the shirtsleeve until my ear was just inches from her mouth.

"Do. You. Have. Any. Idea. How. Worried. I've. Been?"

The words came out like a machine-gun blast. She opened her mouth to continue, but I was way ahead of her. I pulled her aside, by my own shirtsleeve.

"Charlotte, I am a DISGRACE!"

Charlotte opened her mouth to disagree with me, registered what I'd said, and closed her mouth.

"I've come to Paris completely unprepared! I've relied on you for all my knowledge and allowed myself to remain ignorant! The only French words I can remember are ones I can't use in conversation! I haven't so much as glanced at a map! I LOST my information packet before we even left America! And I don't know the address of the VEI!"

Charlotte's eyebrows shot up at that last part. I rapidly

left the Admission of Wrongdoing portion of my speech behind and proceeded to my Humble Request for Forgiveness.

"I am CONSTANTLY taking advantage of your superb organization, your intelligence, and your sense of responsibility, Charlotte. You are right about me not being detail oriented. I am detail DISoriented. And it's going to stop RIGHT NOW!"

Charlotte scowled at me for a good five or ten seconds before shaking her head in disgust and perhaps a wee portion of affection.

"Honestly, Lily, you're going to turn me into a nut job," she said.

I shook my head in disbelief at my own level of moronification and turned both my palms toward the ceiling in an expression of self-disappointment.

"Where's Bonnie?" I asked, in a shameless bid for an Abrupt Subject Change.

Charlotte jerked her thumb in the direction of the crowd.

"Getting an up-close look," she replied. Then she leaned in and whispered, "We think she may have recognized somebody from one of the portraits back in Flemish Seventeenth-century Oils and Watercolors. How did you find us, anyway? This place is gargantuan."

"Oh my God! Lewis! He text messaged me all the way up from reception!"

I looked around for Lewis, but I couldn't pick him out of the *Mona Lisa*–admiring crowd.

"Text messaged you?" asked Charlotte, incredulous. She was well aware of the technical backwardness of the entire Blennerhassett clan.

I glanced over my shoulder and spotted Lewis standing by the window, peering at his Sidekick.

"Be right back," I said to Charlotte. Then I quickly made my way over to Lewis.

"Lewis Pilsky, you are a god among men," I said dramatically.

Lewis looked up at me, and his face turned a remarkable shade of crimson.

"Oh, well . . . you know."

"You SAVED me," I said, waggling my eyebrows for emphasis.

"Oh, well," he repeated. "How did you end up finding your way to the museum?"

I won't tell you I wasn't tempted. Every cell in my body—every single strand of DNA—was silently screaming "LINDY SLOANE SHOWED ME THE WAY!" Instead of replying, though, I let a few heartbeats pass while I thought of a technically honest yet completely discreet response.

"You know, I ended up just asking somebody," I said. "And they turned out to be American and basically gave me door-to-door service."

Lewis nodded and continued to look embarrassed.

"I have COMPLETELY REVISED my feelings on portable communications technology," I said earnestly. Before Lewis could nod or say "oh, well" again, I sensed a looming presence. I felt like a chipmunk that has just noticed a hawk circling overhead.

"Leelee!" said Madame Chavotte. "Are you also seek wees ze stomak big?"

WHAT? Was Madame Chavotte accusing me of being FAT?

"Ze stomak big? Like Teem? Always, your frenz say you are running to ze bassroom. Every time I am looking for you, again, you are in ze bassroom. I am afraid we will all catch zis terrible stomak big."

"Oh, yeah," I said, rubbing my stomach ruefully. "You know, Madame Chavotte, I think the trouble has, um, passed. I'm feeling much better now."

Madame Chavotte scrutinized me for a moment, her monobrow furrowed. For a moment I was gripped with the fear that the game was up. That Madame Chavotte knew the Truth and was about to bust me. She took a step toward me, and I thought it was entirely possible she was about to put me in handcuffs. Instead, she reached out and pushed my hair out of my face, like my mother sometimes does.

"Zees ees good, zen," she said. "A young girl's first treep to Paree should be full of wonder and *amusement*. It ees sumsing she should remember 'er whole life, *non?* No one should 'ave ze stomak big in Paree. I am glad you are *en bonne santé, ma petite poulette.*"

Wow! Every native of France seemed to recognize my innate Little Chickenness.

"What was that all about?" whispered Charlotte after Madame Chavotte moved out of earshot.

"She was just—she was just making sure I was feeling okay," I said.

"That's because Lewis and I kept telling her that you were in the ladies' room during the head count," Charlotte said, giving me a stern look.

"I've TOTALLY learned my lesson," I declared.

"I've heard that before," Charlotte said, and she linked her arm through mine.

"Allons-y, mes enfants," Madame Chavotte was calling. "We go now to eejeepcheyan *antiquités.*"

Whatever eejeepcheyan on tee kee tay turned out to be, I didn't care. As long as I didn't have to find them by myself, I was happy as a lark.

FROM THE PARISIAN DIARY OF
Lily M. Blennerhassett

Started the day off wonderfully, visiting the 17th century Hôtel de Sens, a scrumptious medieval architectural confection of towers and archways. Partook of the delightful hot beverage chocolat in a café, confirming the reputation of the French as the ultimate purveyors of extraordinary tastes.

It has come to my attention, under the psychological ministrations of Charlotte McGrath, that I have allowed the issue of details to escape my life. It has further occurred to me that my journal entries, while full of whimsical and hopeful observations, have nonetheless excluded certain details not always flattering to this author. With that in mind I am including a Personal Addendum to my journal, NOT for publication in the Mulgrew Sentinel:

Experienced abnormal level of brain rot and displayed intelligence roughly equivalent to a lima bean by getting on the Wrong Train and becoming lost somewhere in the vicinity of the Arc de Triomphe. Displayed outrageous levels of dull wittedness by engaging Kindly Elderly man for directions and having absolutely no ability to communicate in French. Continued acting like an enormous addlepated dunderhead, until two Unnamed Good Samaritans personally escorted

me to the Musée du Louvre, where the kindness
and technological savvy of Lewis Pilsky enabled
me to, forty minutes after the appointed time,
rejoin my group at the fabled oil depiction of that
amused noblewoman known throughout the world
as Mona Lisa.

Paris rocks!

Nine

I had viewed more masterpieces than I ever thought possible in one afternoon. As I lay facedown on my bed on the *deuxième étage* of the VEI, my feet throbbed and felt uncomfortably hot, like they were about to go supernova and splatter carbon and stardust up into the stratosphere.

Bonnie and Janet were napping too, but Charlotte was undefeated by our hours at the Louvre. I could hear her flipping through her guidebook, muttering occasional remarks, and scratching notes with her Bic ballpoint. I could practically hear her brain working as she figured out how many places we could visit during our free afternoon tomorrow. This might be an opportune time to show her I was as good as my word, that I was making an effort to find out *seule* what Paris had to offer, instead of relying on Charlotte to figure it out for me. Using the force of ten oxen, I lifted my head off the pillow and looked over at her.

"Hey, Charlotte," I said.

She peered at me over her glasses, lips still pursed in reading-small-print mode.

"You know what I would really like to see while we're in Paris?"

"What?" Charlotte asked, one eye still on her guidebook.

"The Père Lachaise Cemetery," I replied.

Charlotte gaped at me. I gestured toward my pristine guidebook, which I'd unpacked and leafed through before collapsing on my bed.

Taking advantage of Charlotte's unusually speechless state, I pulled the removable metro map from my guidebook.

"It seems to me that if we get on the eleven train here, at the Hôtel de Ville stop, and transfer here, at République, to the three line, then it's just three stops to Père Lachaise. I know it's a little outside the city center, but I think we could make good time and have a few hours to stroll around."

Bonnie had risen silently to a sitting position on her bed, like the Bride of Frankenstein but, well, more wholesome-looking.

"Père Lachaise?" she asked. "Jim Morrison is buried there! Man, I wouldn't mind visiting the Lizard King."

I knew Jim Morrison was a legendary American rock star who'd died in Paris around thirty years ago, because my father had insisted on educating me in the ways of the fossil rock gods. The Lizard King thing was a mystery, though. Maybe he was one of Bonnie's seventeenth century relatives.

"There's someone there for everyone," I said, sounding like an advertising jingle. "Writers, actors, musicians. Oscar Wilde. Sarah Bernhardt. Chopin!" There WERE some advantages to reading one's guidebook. I'm sure I sounded Supremely Knowledgable.

"I know that," Charlotte said patiently. "I just wasn't aware that YOU knew that."

"Well," I said, fanning myself with the metro map, "I thought it was time I did a little research."

"Interesting," said Charlotte. She arched an eyebrow. I have a theory that Charlotte practices arching her eyebrow in private, in front of the mirror, as a way to convey serious thoughtfulness. I'm totally supportive.

"I'm game," said Bonnie. "Maybe I'll run into some old friends."

Yikes. I hadn't considered any possible paranormal high jinks; that might get creepy. But Charlotte looked

 122

positively enthusiastic. She obviously wanted to encourage me in my new ways.

"I think that's an excellent idea, Lily," Charlotte said. "There's a huge amount of history there."

"It was founded by Napoleon!" I shouted, unable to contain the self-pride in my historical Parisian knowledge.

"I don't want to go to a cemetery," whined Janet, who was sprawled on her bed with one arm dangling over the side. "I want to see the Eiffel Tower! I want to take a cruise on the river Seine! I want to climb the Arc de Triomphe!"

Crapstick. The girls all had to stay together, which meant we had to agree unanimously where to go.

"We're supposed to go to the Eiffel Tower after dinner the night before we go home," I told her. I proudly waved the copy of the trip schedule I had borrowed from Bonnie. "So you'll see it then. It's better at night anyway, according to my guidebook."

"What about the Seine? What about all the little shops on the rue de Rivoli where I can buy French *objets*? What about the men in berets and *les chic Parisiennes*? I mean, actual REAL *chic Parisiennes*."

"Listen," I said, plopping down on Janet's bed next to her. "I bet we could talk Madame Chavotte into showing us the Seine and the rue de Rivoli tonight after dinner. But tomorrow is our last Free Time. Madame Chavotte would definitely never take us to Père Lachaise. So let's go there ourselves and witness a place that's really vital to the history of Paris, that's like, three-dimensional history because all these famous French figures are right there beneath us!"

Janet still looked unconvinced. It was time to play the trump card.

"You know, Edith Piaf is buried there," I said.

Janet sat up with a start.

Jackpot!

To the non-Francophile (read: normal person) the name Edith Piaf probably means nothing. However, I had found a little section on Piaf in my guidebook. To the Franco-obsessed, Edith Piaf was recognized as the greatest popular singer of modern French times. I had learned that she was tiny and sang with a tragically tight vibrato. And she was now dead, obviously. But there were droves who worshiped her like the Sloane Rangers worshiped Lindy. Dear Readers, what could be more a more suitable homage to French culture than shedding a few tears over the grave of Piaf?

"I'll even take your picture by her memorial, as a keepsake," I said. "You'll kick yourself later if you miss the chance. I think it could be very important to you, Jah-nay."

I know, I know. It must have seemed like I was bribing her by pronouncing her name in Franglais, and in part I was. But I had also realized that though I thought it stupid, and superficial, and embarrassingly obvious, this girl wanted to be called Jah-nay. Who was I to judge?

"Well . . ." Janet began tentatively.

"Yes!" cried Bonnie, perched regally on her bed. "I am the Lizard King! I can do ANYTHING!"

I looked at Charlotte in alarm. Bonnie might be having some kind of serious and traumatic spontaneous past-life regression. But Charlotte's expression was nothing but happy.

"Well done, Lily," said Charlotte. "Welcome to Paris."

When it came down to it, I surprised myself and everyone else by suggesting we ask the boys if they wanted to join us. I had no personal interest in watching Chaz and Bud toss a football between headstones, but I did feel it would make a big difference to Lewis if we asked him to come along. As for the Mysterious Tim, since he had miraculously "recovered" from his *stomak big*, it might do him some good to see people having a good time around him and with him, even though they didn't know the identity of his older sister. He would see I was as good as my word.

There was a little grumbling, particularly from Janet, who somehow felt the presence of American boys at any

Parisian landmark was unattractive and counterproductive and would detract from her experience. Bonnie, as always, was up for anything. So the invitation was extended and accepted, and after spending a morning with Madame Chavotte touring the modern glass cake of the Bastille Opera House, and lunching on peanut butter sandwiches at the VEI, we were ready for an adventure.

I am pleased and proud to report that the metro directions I had put together were accurate (though I'm certain Charlotte checked them over and discreetly supervised our every step). We came out of the metro onto a quiet, wide street with cobblestone sidewalks and smaller versions of the rounded beige buildings I'd gotten used to in Paris. We walked through the open gateway and it felt like we'd stepped into Wonderland.

"Man, it's like the inner city of the departed," said Bonnie. "Get a load of that energy shift."

I don't know about an energy shift, but I could see right away what Bonnie meant by an inner city. It was like this separate miniature metropolis within Paris. Paved paths went off in every direction, and each one was lined with memorials and mausoleums. Some of them were simple stones, some were elaborate sculptures, and others looked like little houses. There was a strange hush over the place. Even Bud and Chaz were walking quietly ahead of us, though periodically one of them would suddenly lunge back and pantomime hurling a touch-down pass to a phantom quarterback.

"Where's the Famous People Section?" asked Janet.

"Well," I replied patiently, "I don't think there's any one section for them, Janet. I think they're probably scattered individually throughout the grounds."

Janet looked appalled.

"But there must be *thousands* of graves here," she said. "Where do they give out maps? How are we going to find Edith Piaf?"

"And Jim Morrison," added Bonnie, holding her hands palms downward over a small grave marker.

Tim shot us a look. "Wait. Jim Morrison? As in The Doors? Jim Morrison is buried HERE?" he cried.

I had never seen him so animated.

"Yeah, man. Definitely," said Bonnie, looking at Tim with a new level of interest. "Morrison died in Paris, dude. They buried him right here."

Tim seemed momentarily paralyzed with reverence. I was both surprised and impressed. Did other people's fathers also lecture them on fossil rock gods of the past? I would have pegged Tim as more of a Green Day fan.

"Jim Morrison? That is pretty cool. Let's find him!" Lewis said, powering up his Sidekick.

Lewis knew him too?

"Oh, yeah, we have to find him, definitely," said Tim.

"I agree, bro," Bonnie said. She peered over Lewis's

shoulder. "Whaddyagot?"

"Give me a minute," said Lewis, tapping the buttons. "The Internet has never failed me."

"Yo, dawg, what's the delay?" shouted Chaz or Bud, I'm not sure which. (I don't think I could identify one from the other in a court of law.)

"We're trying to find Jim Morrison," I called back.

Bud and Chaz regarded each other.

"Is he in our class?" one of them asked.

I took a brief moment to deliver a silent prayer that neither Bud nor Chaz would ever hold a position of authority in the U.S. government.

Lewis suddenly made a sound indicating some kind of victory (or maybe a spider had crawled into his sleeve). Charlotte and Bonnie were firmly planted at Lewis's shoulder, watching his Sidekick with apparent fascination. Tim (I no longer thought of him as the Mysterious Tim) was standing off to one side, hands thrust into his jeans pockets, as usual.

"Tim," I said, "you have to see what Lewis can do with this thing."

Tim, whose face had been completely transformed since the name Jim Morrison was mentioned, joined us. Bonnie squinched closer, allowing him to sidle in and see what Lewis had found.

And what Lewis had found was extraordinary. He had

found a virtual reality map of the cemetery. One half of the screen showed a picture of where we had come in. When Lewis put the cursor on the photograph, it began to rotate, giving the viewer a 360-degree view of the cemetery from the precise spot where we were standing. On the other half of the screen was a map of the cemetery.

"See, that pulsing red dot shows where we are right now," said Lewis, pointing to the map.

We, his audience, were captivated.

"Now look back at the photograph. See how they've superimposed little red arrows on the picture? They show that we can go in any direction from here. Look at this one, to the right."

There was, in fact, a narrow cobblestone road going off to the right of where we were standing.

"Okay, now, watch the photograph," Lewis said. He clicked on the red arrow going to the right. The photograph faded out, and a new photograph appeared. Lewis made it turn 360 degrees again. "This is what we'll see if we go thirty feet in that direction. And look at the map now. See, the red dot has moved, so we know which direction we're moving in."

"How's that gonna get us to Jim Morrison, bro?" asked Bonnie.

Lewis tapped a few buttons.

"Here's an alphabetical list of notable graves," he said. "We'll click on Morrison."

A cross icon on the map blinked off and on in response.

"That's the one," Lewis said. "Now we know how to get there."

"That is unbelievable," said Tim.

Everyone looked at him simultaneously; then everyone looked away. We didn't want Tim to feel self-conscious about speaking. It should look like he'd been doing it all along.

"Who created this?" Tim asked. "Who has that kind of time, to photograph a three-hundred-sixty-degree view from every spot in this graveyard and create a map for it? Some hardcore Morrison fan?"

"I'm going to create sites like this one day," Lewis said shyly. "When I'm out of school."

"Lewis, I feel certain you're going to become world-famous for doing stuff like this," I said with admiration.

Lewis turned the vibrant crimson color again, and he shot a quick glance in Charlotte's direction, like he was checking if she'd heard.

"But what about Edith Piaf?" cried Janet. "Can Lewis's machine find her?"

Lewis hit a few buttons. Another cross pulsed on the map.

"There she is," he said. "But Jim Morrison is closer.

Maybe we should go there first?"

Janet opened her mouth to object, but Charlotte interrupted her.

"Lewis, I say you're IN CHARGE of this expedition," she said.

"I agree," I stated firmly.

"Sounds good to me," Tim said.

"Let's go see the Lizard King, gentlemen," Bonnie cried.

I'd been called almost every male denomination in the world by Bonnie, but never "gentlemen." Paris seemed to be having a genteel effect on her.

Lewis started walking, holding his Sidekick in front of him the way Mr. Spock carries his tricorder while exploring an unknown planet. We filed behind him, not entirely unlike Madeline and the other eleven little girls in two straight lines trailing Miss Clavel. (You see, Dear Readers, everything DOES go back to Madeline in the end.) We followed Lewis along the outer wall of the cemetery, paused when he paused, then followed him left down a little road.

There were so many monuments, large and small, they almost seemed to be on top of one another. I could make out the names on dozens of them just from where I was standing.

"Even if we get to the right spot, how are we going to

find him?" Tim asked. "There's so many different head-stones."

"Look," said Bonnie quietly.

On the wall of a mausoleum someone had spray-painted JIM and a little arrow pointing to the left. Tim drew in his breath in awe.

"That's vandalism!" I said, outraged.

Bonnie linked her arm through mine. "The rules aren't quite the same here, man," she said. "Don't you feel that? Can't you feel all the thousands of people who have been here to pay their respects to Jim?"

I knew that Bonnie meant "feel" like the animal psychic meant it when she investigated the moods of people's pets on Animal Planet. I was a Writer. I didn't consider myself of the Psychic Ilk. I was of the Verbal Ilk. But I did suddenly feel like crying and singing at the same time. I wished Jake were here to see this.

"I heard they have to send police here on Morrison's birthday and the anniversary of his death every year," said Tim, "because the crowds come and they don't want to leave Jim."

"I've heard that too," said Lewis.

Where did these people hear all these things? I had not come across anything like this in *Star* magazine.

Bud and Chaz remained back on the cobblestone path, chatting together and throwing little fake sucker punches at each other, as we picked our way through the graves in the direction the spray-paint arrow had pointed.

"This is creepy," said Janet. But she kept up with us.

"There it is, people," said Bonnie suddenly.

We stopped.

In front of us were a rectangular grave and headstone, surrounded by a low iron fence. A plaque read:

JAMES DOUGLAS MORRISON 1943–1971

My first thought was that the place was totally covered with litter, but when I took a closer look, I realized all the objects on the grave had been placed there with care.

There were candles, wine bottles, flowers, even little framed pictures of Jim Morrison. He had a moody, beautifully angular face framed by loose brown curls. We stood around the grave, looking down in silence.

"You know, I read somewhere there used to be this cat that hung around the grave all the time," said Tim.

Boy, get this guy started and it turns out he has a lot to say.

"And everybody called the cat Jim. You'd come to the grave, and Jim would appear from behind one of the other headstones and start meowing and rubbing your leg."

"I don't like cats," said Janet. An irritating, irrelevant

comment if I ever heard one.

"Where is it then?" I asked, looking around.

"Some fan took him home, in, like, the eighties, they say," replied Tim.

Bonnie suddenly began to sing softly.

This is the end
Beautiful friend . . .

It didn't really surprise me that Bonnie had a lovely voice. It DID surprise me when first Tim, then Lewis began to sing along with her.

I made a mental note to get a Doors CD when I got home. Clearly, this was a phenomenon I needed to investigate more thoroughly.

"People, I'm getting the heebie-jeebies!" cried Janet.

I wasn't happy she'd interrupted the moment, but to be honest, I had goose bumps up and down both arms too.

"We should go," said Lewis.

Bonnie was still humming, her eyes closed, one finger lightly touching the headstone. She had one of those half Buddha smiles on her face.

I looked around at our little group. And a strange little group we were. A Future Corporate Executive, a Reincarnated Medieval Queen, a Francophile, a Computer Geek, an Until Recently Silent Sibling of a Celebrity, and a Writer. I had a feeling this was the moment I would most remember when I passed them in the hall after we were back at school.

"On to Edith Piaf, then," Lewis said, brandishing his Sidekick.

Janet gave a little whoop of happiness.

"Step right this way, ladies and gentlemen," said Lewis.

And we followed him, like obedient little lambs, through the city of the dead.

Ten

It was almost a completely perfect outing. Almost. We were heading through the gate to go back to the metro station when Charlotte realized with dismay that she'd left her camera behind.

"I know exactly where it is," Charlotte said. "I put it down right next to Oscar Wilde."

It figures Charlotte would have become distracted at Oscar Wilde's grave. I suppose it had been my fault, completely. She had tried numerous tactics to get me to walk away. But I had been so completely overcome with awe, I hadn't wanted to leave the grave at all. I kept staring at it, trying to imagine him, Wilde himself, with that Brain and those Hands that had written all that stuff of greatness, right there in the ground below me. And I couldn't help remembering the last thing Wilde supposedly said before he died. It was "Either that wallpaper goes or I do." A genius even as he took his last breath. Who was I kidding? With or without Paris, I was no Oscar Wilde, and never would be. I stood, caught in his spell. Charlotte actually had to walk away to provoke me into leaving. But she had left her camera behind.

Oops.

"You guys go ahead," I said. "I'll go back with Charlotte for the camera, and we'll meet you outside the gates."

I remembered exactly where the Big Monument was. Unfortunately, it was clear on the other side of the cemetery, which was a bit of a hike.

"A little exercise will be good for us," I said to Charlotte as we trotted briskly up the main cemetery road.

"Lily Blennerhassett, you have evolved since we came to Paris," Charlotte said.

I gave her a brilliant smile but saved my breath for important things. Like breathing.

"Finding out about this cemetery, figuring out how to get us all here, that's really great. You're finally taking some responsibility for yourself."

I beamed again. I loved it when Charlotte was proud of me. But I couldn't help thinking at the same time that I'd become exactly what I'd said I would never become. A Simple Tourist.

"Doesn't it feel good? Don't you feel better about yourself?" Charlotte asked.

I sighed, scanning the vista for signs of Wilde.

"Yes, I pretty much do, and yes, you were right about me needing to take control of details and stuff," I said. "As evidenced by the Complete and Utter State of Terror I found myself in when I got on the Wrong Train. I'm never going to let THAT happen to me again."

Charlotte peered at my face as we walked.

"So why do you look . . . less than thrilled?" she asked.

"Oh, I don't know," I said. Which of course means I DO know, but please pull it out of me.

"What?" Charlotte asked.

"I just feel kind of stupid," I said.

"About getting on the Wrong Train?" she asked patiently.

I wondered for how many years THAT was going to keep coming up.

"No. I mean, yes, obviously. But right now I'm talking about . . . you know."

Nice sentence fragment, huh?

"I'm not getting it, Lily," Charlotte said.

I could see Wilde's headstone several yards off now. It was a friendly sight. Even dead, the guy had nice timing.

"*Madeline,*" I said. "I thought coming to Paris would give me my *Madeline.*"

"The cookie?" Charlotte asked.

"The magnum opus," I replied. "*Madeline*. The picture book."

"I LOVE the Madeline books!" Charlotte cried.

"Exactly," I said. "Everyone does. I thought Paris was going to do the same thing for me that it did for Ludwig Bemelmans."

"Your Great Parisian Novel?" Charlotte asked. "What makes you think Paris isn't going to do that for you?"

I sighed and glanced over in the direction of Wilde. We'd arrived at his headstone. Me, author of nothing, contemplating the grave of a literary giant. I imagined a sympathetic vibe transmitting from him to me.

"I really got only one good nugget," I said. "A character like that ditzy designer broad we met who Janet thought was the archetype for Parisian chic. But it was while I was coming up with that character that I got on the Wrong Train. You know, at that point I not only had no idea what metro stop we were at, I'm not even sure I was aware of what planet I was on. And it's fine, actually. I learned my lesson. I need to be a Simple Tourist in Paris. That's okay. I just . . . you know. I thought I was FINALLY going to have something interesting enough to write a book about."

Charlotte picked up her camera and snapped the cover off and on as she thought.

"Lily, if you want to write the Great Parisian Novel,

I'm sure you can. But what makes you think you have to write about Paris to be interesting enough? Why does it *have* to be Paris?"

"Well . . ." I began. "Because it does. I've got to get out and find Exotic Things, things that aren't from my Regular Life, because my Regular Life isn't interesting. No offense," I added, since Charlotte was a central part of my Regular Life.

Charlotte sighed and took my arm.

"Okay. Let me ask you this, Lily. What's your favorite book?"

"You know what my favorite book is. It's *To Kill a Mockingbird*."

"And why is it your favorite book?"

"Because it's the Perfect Novel. It has EVERYTHING."

"Such as?"

"Fascinating characters. Drama. Comedy. Betrayal. Grace."

Charlotte nodded.

"And where does it take place?"

At least she was finally asking some questions I knew the answer to.

"A little town in Alabama. Maycomb."

"And throughout the book do we ever leave this little town?"

I entertained a quick, amusing thought of the Finch

family traveling to Paris.

"Nope," I answered.

"Nope," Charlotte repeated. "Because it wasn't necessary. The writer—"

"Harper Lee," I interrupted, because it was nice to know something every once in a while.

"—because Harper Lee knew she didn't *need* to go to Timbuktu to write a novel. She wrote about a town like the one she lived in, about a childhood similar to her own, about regular people who resembled people she knew. She took what she knew from her own life, and she created something spectacular."

"But Charlotte, I'm not Harper Lee," I said.

"No, you're not. You're Lily Blennerhassett."

Hey.

HEY!

I'd kind of FORGOTTEN about that! Like Harper Lee, I live in a small, ordinary town. But I am not a small, ordinary person! I am Lily Blennerhassett. And I always will be. And whether I am wrestling with a great white shark off the coast of Tasmania or eating broiled free-range turkey on whole grain bread at home, I am going to write good books. Because it wasn't about Paris.

It was about Me.

I looked at Charlotte and wondered if it was a burden to be Right All the Time, as she was.

"You're right," I said. "Again. AGAIN. Is there ANY-THING you don't know the answer to? Not that I'm complaining, mind you, but is there really anything you don't know about?"

It was supposed to be a rhetorical question, but Charlotte appeared to be mulling it over carefully.

"Boys. I don't really know anything about boys, Lily," she said. "I know there was a lot of . . . um, confusion last year with The Boy and Jake. But you muddled through it. You actually have a boyfriend now! I can't help thinking sometimes that I never will."

"Of course you will," I said.

"It's statistically quite unlikely," said Charlotte.

I don't know where she got her statistics (probably *The Wall Street Journal*), but I was suddenly determined that Charlotte WOULD have a boyfriend.

And then I had a Small Burst of Brain.

"What about Lewis?" I asked. Sure, he was short, but so was Charlotte. They both were really smart. They both were studious and goodhearted. They both seemed to know exactly what they wanted to do with their lives.

"What about him?" Charlotte asked. But she knew perfectly well what I meant. Her face had turned red. Oscar Wilde must have been having a field day watching this.

"He's completely revised my thinking on computer dudes, you know," I said. "I told you, he took it upon himself to text message me when I was lost. He's the one who got me to where the group was in the Louvre. Lewis, like, saved me. And that virtual tour thing of the cemetery he found and figured out how to use—that was remarkable. You have to admit it. He's not your run-of-the-mill guy."

I snuck a quick look at Charlotte's face. She was doing the eyebrow arch thing, but she was directing it at one of her shoelaces.

"I don't know, Lily," she said finally.

"Charlotte, I'm not asking you to MARRY him. I'm just saying, you know. Keep it somewhere in the back of your mind. He could be Boyfriend Material. And remember, I AM an expert."

I knew well enough to quit while I was ahead. I initiated an Abrupt Subject Change.

"It's getting late," I said. "It's already six and aren't we supposed to meet back at the VEI before dinner, at seven?"

"Yes," said Charlotte, looking relieved to have a new topic of conversation. "We'll have just enough time. Come on."

I blew Oscar a kiss good-bye, and we did the little half-jog thing down the central path. Eventually I could see the main gates ahead of us, and I felt relieved that we were almost there.

But something looked wrong.

As we got closer and closer to the gates, it registered in my brain that they were, indeed, GATES. They were tall gates, and those tall gates were CLOSED. The Père Lachaise Cemetery had been locked up tighter than Willy Wonka's Chocolate Factory after the Oompa Loompas were hired.

"Good grief, we're locked in!" I cried.

Charlotte skidded to a stop next to me, unusually silent.

"We're locked in!" I repeated.

We could see the road and the sidewalk just through the gates. But these were serious can't-be-climbed, can't-be-gotten-around gates. These gates meant Business.

"There must be SOMEONE around," Charlotte said. "These gates can't have been locked for more than a few minutes. Where did our friends go? They were supposed to wait for us right outside the gates."

We called HELLO in every direction, but no guard appeared. However, Lewis, Tim, and Janet did appear on the other side of the fence. A moment later Bonnie appeared as well.

"There you guys are," Lewis said. "Did you find the camera? We gotta motivate. Hey, is this thing locked?"

"Honestly, girls, what are you doing?" Janet called. "You aren't supposed to be in there anymore. The cemetery is *fermé* for the evening."

"If you knew they were locking the gates, why didn't

you stop them?" I hissed at Jah-nay.

"We didn't know, man," Bonnie said, staring up at the pointy tops of the gate. "We were sitting on some benches down the street."

"You girls better do something, *tout de suite*, before they let out *les chiens de garde*," said Janet.

Everybody, on both sides of the gate, froze.

"What did you say?" I asked.

Janet, I fear with some evident satisfaction, pointed to a sign mounted on one of the gates. It read:

ATTENTION—CHIENS DE GARDE

"Guard dogs?" yelled Tim, getting an A for accuracy in Spontaneous French Sign Translation. "They've got guard dogs on duty in there? You guys have got to get out right now!"

Nice. Evening was approaching. We were locked in the inner city of the living dead. And any moment now we were likely to be approached by a salivating German shepherd with an antisocial canine personality disorder.

"Lewis!" Charlotte cried. "Think! There must be SOMETHING! If anyone can get us out of here, you can!"

For the third time in so many days Lewis spontaneously went crimson in the face and neck. I think, actually, this might have been his most significant blush yet. He whipped out his Sidekick and began to type.

It was around then that Chaz and Bud showed up, taking in our situation with a staccato stream of laughter.

"Climb it!" cried Bud. Or Chaz.

"We can't climb it. It's too slick and too high, and there's pointy things at the top," Charlotte said. "There's nothing to get a grip with."

Which was exactly what I needed to do at that moment. Get a grip.

"No, seriously, just climb it," repeated Chaz. Or Bud. "We climb over locked gates all the time."

"Well, we don't," I said.

Lewis seemed to have found something on the computer.

"I don't think text messaging is going to help when we're being torn limb from limb by the rabid French *Chiens* of the Dead," I said. Charlotte shushed me.

"Okay, I've found a phone number on a tourist website," Lewis said. "I can call it on my cell, but I might not be able to get them to understand me. Who speaks the best French?"

"Jah-nay," said Charlotte and I simultaneously.

Janet looked triumphantly pleased. She clasped her hands together and pressed them to her heart. But before she could deliver an acceptance speech, I interrupted.

Well-timed flattery could be a highly effective tool.

"Yep, nobody can speak French better than Jah-nay. Did you dial, Lewis? Is it ringing? Are you ready, Jah-nay? Any second now."

Lewis held up one finger. He was holding his cell phone to his ear. Then suddenly, as if he'd just discovered it was a hand grenade, he waved it in Janet's face. She took the phone quickly, and put it to her ear.

"*Allô, oui? Je m'appelle Jahnay, et je suis une américaine qui visité le Cimetière Père Lachaise. Maintenant mes deux amies sont accidentellement fermées dedans. . . . Oui? . . . Oui? . . . Formidable, merci bien.*"

Wow. She spoke French as well as Lindy Sloane. I didn't remember her speaking that well before. Had Janet been using her time in Paris to practice her French?

Janet put her hand over the phone. "The security office is nearby. Someone is coming out."

Sure enough, Charlotte and I heard footsteps behind us. A tired, bored-looking man in a guard's uniform approached us, shaking his head in disgust.

"I'm so sorry!" I cried. "We ran back for my friend's camera, and when we came back, the gates were locked."

The man ignored me, pulling a key from a large chain he wore around his waist.

"We told them to just climb over it," called Chaz or Bud.

The guard hesitated, squinting through the gate and sizing up the Football Twins.

"Climbing ees streectly forbeeden," he said, scowling. "Ees for to go to jail."

"We never intended to climb," Charlotte said.

"They're something of a pair of dunderheads," I added.

The guard unlocked the gate and opened it enough for Charlotte and me to scamper through. We all began saying thank you at the same time. Janet, I'm sorry to say, was the only one with both the presence of mind and the elementary good breeding to say it in French.

"Merci bien, monsieur!" she practically cooed.

The guard paused and looked at Janet.

"Il n'ya pas de quoi, petite demoiselle. J'espère que ta voyage est bien agréable."

"Oh, *merci bien!*" cried Janet. The guard walked slowly and sadly, a bit like Eyeore from *Winnie the Pooh*, back to whatever office he'd magically appeared from.

"We'd better move if we're going to get back to the VEI on time," I said.

"Does anyone know where we're supposed to have dinner?" asked Tim.

"I think we're supposed to pick. Madame Chavotte said it was our last night here, so we could have the kind of meal we wanted."

"Italian," said Tim.

"Burgers," said Bud (or Chaz).

"Sushi," said Bonnie.

"Jah-nay is the hero of the hour," I said. "I think she ought to pick where we're going to eat."

Janet practically quivered with happiness.

"Oh, Lily, that's so *agréable* of you. I do know a place. I know *just* the place."

This time I would be sure to write down both the name and address of the restaurant we were going to beforehand. Just in case. And I had of course drummed into my memory banks the location of the VEI. It was, with the Perfection of the Universe's Touch, located on the Rue Charlot.

Looked like Charlotte Street to me.

Eleven

True to her Francophilian form, Janet had found us a restaurant that looked directly onto the Eiffel Tower. It was a nice little place with outdoor tables, one of which had been set for ten people—especially for us.

"Who's the tenth?" I asked. "There are eight of us, plus Madame Chavotte, if she ever gets here, which makes nine."

I had a brief, surreal flash of hope that Lindy Sloane would be joining us.

"Maybe the spirit of Jim Morrison followed us, and the seat is for him," said Bonnie, sitting down in one of the chairs next to me and folding her legs into her customary lotus dining position.

Charlotte took a seat on my right, and I noticed that

she didn't object when I waved Lewis over to sit on her other side.

"No, this is all wrong!" cried Janet. "It has to be *garçon-fille, garçon-fille.*"

My opinion of Janet had, in fact, improved, but not enough to agree that during our final dinner in France we were required to sit boy-girl, boy-girl.

A dapper-looking man dressed all in white appeared with a stack of menus, which he handed to each of us. Glancing at mine, I felt suddenly as if I had been asked to provide an accurate translation of the glyphs on the Rosetta Stone.

Well, this *was* French food. Presumably, everything would be good. *Abats à l'étouffée*, for example, sounded exciting.

"Do you know what *abats* is?" I asked Charlotte.

Charlotte had a miniature French-English dictionary, which she produced from her purse.

"Organ meats," she said.

Ew.

I was feeling adventurous, but I didn't want to eat anything's liver or spleen, no matter how much mouth-watering sauce it was covered in. I scanned the menu for another interesting word.

"What about *civelles*?" I asked. This one took Charlotte longer to find.

"Baby eel," she replied.

Heaven forfend! Didn't they have anything made by Chef Boyardee?

"Look for *boeuf, poulet,* and *poisson,*" Charlotte said with confidence.

"Because . . ."

"Because they are beef, chicken, and fish," Charlotte replied.

Now we were talking! Though I might stay away from the chicken, having acquired a new affection for all things *poulette.*

Lewis leaned around Charlotte and tapped me on the shoulder.

"What do you usually like, Lily?" he asked. "I found a French cuisine translation site on my Sidekick."

"Well . . . ," I said. "Do the French make tacos?"

"Not unless they're under protest," Lewis said. "What about steak? Salmon?"

"Salmon!" I cried.

Lewis made some entries.

"How does the Sidekick know what restaurant we're at?" I asked.

"It doesn't. I input the entries on this menu that have the word *salmon,* and it's translating them."

Paris was a beautiful world with Lewis in it.

"What about poached salmon with a light hollandaise

sauce garnished with sorrel and served with sautéed slices
of potatoes and a green salad with walnuts?" he asked.

"I'll take it!" I exclaimed with delight. Lewis pointed to
the entry on my menu where it was written in French. I
beamed with satisfaction.

"Charlotte, did you see what Lewis just did?"

Charlotte turned and gave me a look of innocent surprise that, and I mean this in the nicest possible way,
looked Really Fake. I KNEW IT! Charlotte thought I
was right: Lewis might, in fact, be Boyfriend Material for
her.

"Lewis, Charlotte loves steak. Can you make your
Sidekick find her a good dish?"

"I'm getting steak too," Lewis said.

Charlotte and Lewis glanced at each other, then quickly
looked away, then looked back again. I could swear that,
just for a second as their heads bent together over the
Sidekick, a few cartoon bluebirds circled over them,
whistling an Edith Piaf tune. But it might just have been
the light.

I wanted to ask Bonnie what she was getting, but she
was deep into a conversation with Tim that was touching
on the post-Doors career of a keyboardist named Ray
Manzarek. I waited patiently while several tragically short
fossil rock lives, including those of a Janis Joplin, a Jimi
Hendrix, and a Keith Sun or Moon—I can't remember

which—were gravely discussed. Lewis momentarily interrupted to tell Bonnie and Tim not to forget Brian Jones. The conversation was substantially out of my league. Even Bud and Chaz were thoroughly immersed, though not in words. They had fashioned a miniature soccer field out of their silverware and were shooting goals at each other with ice cubes.

Janet, meanwhile, had taken hold of the arm of a passing waiter, and in spite of his Herculean efforts to speak to her in English, she was insisting that their exchange be entirely in French. When he finally managed to wiggle free, Janet turned back to the table with her hands clasped triumphantly under her chin.

"I'm having the house special," she declared, with all the import of a celebrity announcing the winner of the Best Actor Oscar.

"What is the special?" asked Lewis.

"Cervelles de veau provençale," Janet said, smacking her lips theatrically.

"Which is . . . ," I prompted.

"The house special!" Janet declared.

She was distracted by the passing of a busboy, whom she physically detained as she described, in French, her need for a Diet Coke with lemon.

"Hey, Lewis. Let me see that a sec," I whispered.

Lewis passed his Sidekick. Charlotte looked at it first,

then grimly handed it my way.

In the search field of his French cuisine translator, Lewis had typed "Cervelles de veau provençale."

In the English description field blinked the words *Calf brains with black olives*.

Phletamgah.

I WAS going to tell her. Really and honestly and truly, my intention was to tell Janet what the translation said, just to make sure it was actually her intention to order cow brains for dinner.

But just before I got to it, I happened to glance down the sidewalk.

If there was such a thing as a picture dictionary, and you looked up "Hot French Guy," THIS man's picture would have been shown as the definition. He was tall and dark, with black hair turning gray at the temples, high cheek-bones, and perfectly shaped eyebrows arched over chocolate brown eyes. He was dressed so neatly, he might have just tumbled out of the window display of a department store. He wore pleated white pants and a pale-blue cotton shirt, over which he had casually draped a cardigan sweater so that it hung neatly from his shoulders. His shoes looked as if they'd just been unwrapped from tissue paper and lifted out of their box. Under one arm he carried a little leather bag that I would not DREAM of calling a man purse. He walked confidently and easily, as if the city belonged to him.

My heart leaped into my mouth when he stopped at our café. Now, let me be completely clear. My heart belongs to Jake. But that happy fact did not, COULD not, distract me from this man-tastic creature. I had never seen anyone so perfect-looking up close. And he was getting closer. Was he coming HERE? I had a brief sense of a larger, older, dowdier person behind him. Must be his mother, I thought.

"And 'ere we are, my leetle birds. I am mortified to be late!" called a dreadfully familiar voice.

I saw with shock and dismay that Madame Chavotte seemed to be trying to push her way past Hot French Guy to get to our table. I turned red with embarrassment. Madame Chavotte kept charging toward us as if Hot French Guy weren't even there. He moved just ahead of her, as if she'd stuck a snow shovel under him and was plowing him along.

"*Bon*, good, I see we are just een time to order, *non*?"

Madame Chavotte sat down in one of the empty chairs and patted the seat of the other with her hand.

You can imagine my general state of discombobulation when Hot French Guy sat down next to her at OUR table. Janet's eyes almost popped out of her head. (Mine, I'm sure, behaved much more discreetly.)

"Everywahn, zees ees my baby brudder, Louis-Marc," said Madame Chavotte, beaming.

The entire science of genetics, at least in my mind, became instantaneously invalid. This—this Franco Adonis was directly related to my Burly Teacher?

Hot French Guy flashed a million-dollar smile.

"He does not speak much of ze English, so we will all 'ave to practice our best French, *oui*? Eet ees like a pop quiz for ze last night."

"Radical," murmured Bonnie.

"You can pliz forgive me for bringing 'eem, but I only get to see my leetlest brudder once a year," Madame Chavotte said, flagging down a waiter and gesturing at the menu. Hot French Guy flashed his smile again and punctuated it with a wink.

I forgave her.

Hot French Guy and I were not destined to exchange any conversation during our dinner. In fact, sitting in between his sister and Janet, HFG seemed content to chat with them. And I grudgingly admit that in spite of the Overwhelming Number of Irritating Characteristics that Janet possessed, she kept her cool in the face of Parisian hotness and, from what I could tell, held up her end of the conversation pretty well.

It was actually turning out to be a quiet, introspective meal for me altogether. Bonnie and Tim had apparently returned in their discussion to the birth of Elvis and were slowly working their way forward through three decades of ensuing rock-and-roll development. Lewis and Charlotte seemed to be having an enthusiastic exchange concerning the effect of the Internet on the world business community. Bud (or possibly Chaz) scored an ice cube goal and was doing a victory dance with the salt shaker. So I just sat back and soaked up the Frenchness that lay in the streets all around me. Happy to be a Simple Tourist in the crowd.

Soaring in the distance, the Eiffel Tower glittered like an eccentric jewel. Though my French hadn't improved greatly, the sounds of the language everywhere had become comfortingly familiar. The quaint, tidy streets were beginning to feel like home.

It was almost impossible to believe that tomorrow we would be going home. I did miss my family, but I wished they could simply come to me. I imagined my beagle, Milo, racing down the Rue de Rivoli, wearing a jaunty canine beret and gripping a baguette in his jaws. I could see my father behind the wheel of a little French Renault, meticulously maintaining the speed limit in kilometers. My mother would carry an enormous guidebook and stop to personally thank every uniformed *agent de police* she passed. And Jake, aglow in the Parisian evening light, clutching a single red rose. . . .

I felt like I had only just begun to truly experience Paris, had just started to really appreciate it, and I was being whisked back home to the Land of Big and Plenty, where the ninth grade loomed before me like a lengthy, multifaceted obstacle course.

I remained quiet, listening to my friends chatter and watching the splendor of Paris, until I had completely devoured every last morsel of my salmon. When the plates were cleared away, Madame Chavotte stood up and raised her glass.

"*Mes enfants . . .*" she began, her eyebrow quivering with emotion. "We 'ave come almoss to ze end of our French *voyage*. For een ze regular times, I am ze guest een your country, and you are ze ones at 'ome. For ze lass five days, eet ees you who 'ave been ze guests, and I 'ave been ze one at home. Eet 'ess geeven me great plizure, *mes enfants*, to 'ave you een my 'ome. You 'ave made Madame Chavotte proud, and you 'ave been very good *représentants* of United States and of Mulgrew School. Per'aps you take a leetle of Paris 'ome wiz you. And I am so plizzed to see dat some of you are already a leetle leeving *commes les français*, like *ma petite* Jah-nay, yes?"

At being singled out as acting *commes les français*, Janet sat up straight in her chair and practically erupted into flaming lava streams of pride. She shot a quick look at Hot French Guy, who flashed his superstar smile.

"*Oui, oui, vraiment*, 'ow she speak ze French wiz my

brudder so well, yes? 'Ow she 'as arranged ze scarf around 'er neck juss so."

Janet adjusted her new scarf modestly.

"And 'ow she eat *commes les français*, too, non? Ze Bud and ze Chaz 'ave 'amburgers, I can't beliv it! In *Paree*, to eat ze burgers!"

Bud and Chaz grinned and looked thoroughly un-ashamed.

"But Jah-nay, she 'ave ze palate *sophistiqué*! Most Americans will not touch ze *cervelles*. Jah-nay, she under-stand not to pass up a famous delicacy only because it ees cow brain!"

As Madame Chavotte paused to recollect her thoughts, I watched the color drain from Janet's face with alarming swiftness.

"*Où est la toilette?*" she whispered at a nearby waiter, who did not or chose not to hear her.

"*Où est la toilette?*" she said to Hot French Guy, who shrugged magnificently.

Another waiter carrying a pitcher of water attempted to pass behind Janet's chair. She leaped to her feet and grabbed him, one fist on each side of his collar.

"*Où est la toilette!*" she snarled.

The waiter, alarmed, pointed in the direction of the bathroom. Janet grabbed the pitcher of water from his hands, took a long guzzle, and sprinted to the bathroom as if she were attempting to qualify for the Olympic track and field team. Madame Chavotte watched Janet without comment, but looking at her very closely, I saw what appeared to be a mischievous twinkle in her eye. Was the platoon sergeant–like Madame Chavotte, the glowering monobrowed bastion of Nonhumor, having a little fun at Janet's expense? I felt a sudden blossoming of affection for my French teacher. She saw me looking at her, and she might possibly have given me a little wink. Or maybe it was just a nervous tic.

After the bathroom door had slammed, and the subdued giggles issuing from Some of Us Who Shall Remain Nameless had faded, Madame Chavotte continued speaking as if nothing had happened.

"Okay, zen, we are livving for ze airport early in ze morning, so mek sure to get plenty of sleep. Since we 'ave so much time on ze plane, I am asking each one of you to write a t'ree-'undred-word essay on 'ow ze veezeet to Paris 'as changed you. I will collect zem when we have landed in ze U.S."

There was a chorus of groans and protests, its epicenter being with Bud and Chaz. I, on the other hand, found myself kind of looking forward to the exercise. Because through all my phases and dramatic episodes, I am and always will be Lily Blennerhassett, Writer Extraordinaire.

And so, even as the lights of Paris blaze and twinkle outside, we have come to the final evening of our journey. We spent our last day, in what I consider a poetically fitting manner, strolling amongst the memorials to some of Paris's most esteemed citizens and expatriates. While paying homage to these honorable achievers of days gone by, we took the time to contemplate our own mortality as well as we wandered down the avenues of eternity.

Also, at dinner Janet ate cow brains and hurled.

Twelve

All the way to the airport, I tried to absorb my last glimpses of Paris and imprint them into my brain. The boutiques and outdoor cafés, the petit bakeries emitting scents of croissants and coffee, the mysterious gated archways leading to courtyards. It was all there, right before my eyes. But in less than twenty-four hours I would be back on American roads, passing city-size Home Depots and highway billboards enticing travelers to visit the local Chuck E. Cheese.

Madame Chavotte, not unlike my father, was ruthlessly efficient when it came to travel, and she made sure we arrived at the airport several hours before our plane was scheduled to board. Though buzzing with an international cast, Charles de Gaulle Airport still had a distinctly

French flavor. It inspired me to buy a *Paris-Match* magazine, an oversized colorful French publication that is a kind of hybrid of *People* magazine and *Newsweek*, with a teeny bit of *Star* magazine for good measure.

But none of us were allowed to linger and shop for long. Madame Chavotte herded us like a flock of untrustworthy sheep toward our gate. There was a brief drama when Janet discovered she had left her boarding pass and passport balanced on top of the toilet paper dispenser in the ladies' room approximately six miles back down the corridor. We all had to jog in tandem back to the spot. I like to think we looked like the cast of *CSI* filming a promo: important, mysterious, and undoubtedly in One Serious Hurry. In spite of the unscheduled expedition, we managed to find ourselves seated at the gate with a tight window of just 109 minutes to spare.

Bonnie immediately folded herself into the lotus position and disappeared into her Interior Universe, where passports and boarding calls were not required. Janet was a far cry from the effervescent *French Women Don't Get Fat*–wielding enthusiast she'd been on the trip over. She had not completely recovered from her foray into the world of French delicacies the night before and definitely looked a little green around the gills as she sucked weakly on a Coke (full strength). Tim was slouched down in his seat and had fired up his iPod. He had the volume turned up so high, I could identify the band (The Wallflowers) and the tune ("Everybody Out of the Water") from a distance of eleven feet. Bud and Chaz had spotted two tourists wearing Yankees shirts, and the four of them were shouting cheerfully about batting averages. Charlotte was already working on her essay. She sat next to Lewis, who was peering intently at his Sidekick. Even when they weren't talking, they looked like they were.

"What's the haps, Lew?" I asked, pointing to the Sidekick, where I could tell without looking that he was perusing news headlines.

"Yesterday they released four giant catfish into a Cambodian river in an attempt to repopulate the species," he replied.

"No, they did not!" I said enthusiastically. "Can you check the entertainment headlines?"

Lewis hit a few buttons.

"'Houston Ramada accidentally walks out of Bloomingdale's with $1,800 of lip care products in her bag,'" he read.

"Well, that was bound to happen sooner or later," I said. "Anything else?"

"Your homegirl Lindy Sloane got in trouble for disappearing from her movie set."

"It was a family thing," I stated.

Lewis glanced up at me.

"What do you mean, it was a family thing? That's not what it says here."

Oops.

"I mean . . . that'd be my best guess. That it was some family thing. Keep reading," I said.

"'Sloane was mobbed by reporters and paparazzi in Charles de Gaulle Airport on Tuesday'—hey, that's here, she was right here yesterday!" he interjected. "'Her publicist denied that her disappearance was unauthorized and explained that her client had been advised by both the film's director and her personal team of physicians to take a few days of rest and relaxation after suffering from an exhaustive bout of a stomach virus.'"

"Actually, I'm here on the advice of my personal physicians too," I quipped. Lewis kept reading.

"'Sloane herself then interrupted to confirm her publicist's story. She added, "I took some time to recuperate by taking long walks along the Champs-Elysées, and thank God I did! While I was there, I found a little American girl who had gotten separated from her group and was lost! The little girl was terrified, but of course she was quite excited to recognize me, and being a fan, she trusted me right away. With the help of some of my staff, I was able to get her back to her people. I'm so grateful I was in the right place at the right time. A little girl wandering alone in the streets of Paris might have ended tragically if it hadn't been for my intervention.'" That's the end of the article."

A little American girl? She was talking about ME! I could accept being called a Little Chicken by a Kindly Elderly Parisian Gentleman. But Lindy Sloane, who arguably had not eaten a sandwich in fifteen months and had a head and body combo that looked like a giant meatball perched atop a single strand of spaghetti, calling ME a little girl?

I was OUTRAGED. I opened my mouth to tell Lewis the entire *Star* magazine–level outrageous story. But over his shoulder I caught a glimpse of Tim drumming his carry-on bag and moving his lips to the Wallflowers. He glanced up at me, flashed me a thumbs-up sign, and resumed his drumming.

I closed my mouth. I had the gossip anecdote of a lifetime, and I was keeping it to myself.

Sometimes it is so difficult being me, Lily M. Blennerhassett. But I wouldn't swap it for love or money.

Lewis continued to browse the headlines. "A woman found a severed finger in her bowl of chili at Wendy's,'" he read.

Three seats away, Janet overheard and uttered a little shriek. Moments later she was on her feet and frantically querying other passengers for the location of the nearest *toilette*.

But these amusing interludes could not suitably alleviate

the boredom I was experiencing. You see, when you are GOING somewhere and you arrive in the airport, you are THERE. But when you are LEAVING someplace and you are waiting in the airport, you are neither HERE nor THERE. Charles de Gaulle Airport wasn't Paris; it wasn't really even France (except technically, and geographically, and legally). It was a hub of arriving and departing humanity where boredom reigned. Time had slowed to a Ridiculous Extent. I was so bored that I even skimmed the entire volume of *French Women Don't Get Fat*. When I finished, I began to look at my watch every two minutes, making note of my surroundings (though at this point my Mental Pool was overflowing and required No Further Details of Any Kind).

Minute Two: Svelte woman in highly tailored suit and scary heels wearing expensive accessories strides past our gate, trailing a good sixteen inches of toilet paper behind one shoe.

Minute Four: Blond Demon Child by window demands attention from Weary Mother. Receiving none, she hurls herself to the floor, shrieks, and points to her mother while shouting, "Mommy pushed me!"

Minute Six: Businessman standing by pay phones drops his plastic container of strawberry Yoplait, which shatters and splatters pink goo everywhere. Businessman departs hastily. Janet runs back to the *toilette*.

Minute Eight: Young, badly dressed Houston Ramada wannabe pauses near gate, loudly talking on her cell phone. All airport noise, including landing and takeoff sounds, are briefly drowned out by the following: "So I'm all like . . . what? And he's all like . . . no, you did not! And I'm all like . . . so what if I did? And he's all like . . . later. And I'm all like . . . whatever, loser!" Young, badly dressed Houston Ramada wannabe's cell phone battery suddenly dies, and her conversation is cut short. Several passengers seated nearby are all like . . . YAY!

Minute Ten: Madame Chavotte falls asleep, her mouth wide open in a menacing, scarlet *O*.

Minute Twelve: They are coming to take me away. Actually, they are coming to take us all away. Two very neat men in pilot's uniforms are strolling toward our gate. They look jovial but focused. Energetic but centered. French but not French. They are pulling two identical black suitcases behind them. They are wearing identical sunglasses and sport identical clipped beards. Golden wing pins gleam from their chests. The Pilot Twins stop briefly to exchange words with the flight attendant on duty, who gazes at them with liquid, adoring eyes. Then the door with the sign that says DO NOT ENTER in six or eight languages opens, and the Pilot Twins go through. One of them glances over his shoulder, seemingly at me (it's hard to be precise with the sunglasses). Like he's telling me to get it together, because this is it.

Then they both disappeared through the Do Not Enter door. Not a few seconds later we heard the official boarding call, first in French, then in English.

"It's time," said Charlotte in her Scout leader kind of way. "Everybody stow your stuff in your carry-ons, and make sure you have your passports out, because they're going to want to see them when we board."

Apparently I did not move fast enough.

"Come on, people!" cried Charlotte. "Continents drift faster than this!"

Madame Chavotte was standing behind Charlotte, waving her arms the way those guys in the jumpsuits and headphones who stand out on the runway do when they want to tell the plane where to go.

"Mek a line 'ere be'ind me," she was calling. And though nobody seemed to move, we were suddenly more or less in a line behind her. She was just That Big, I figured.

When the line started to move, I felt an unexpected surge of panic. I gripped at Charlotte's shirt in front of me.

"Charlotte," I whispered, "I don't want to go!"

Charlotte nodded.

"No, I mean I really, really don't want to go! I'm not ready. I CAN'T LEAVE!"

I was getting to a place that might be called pre-pre-hysterical. Then I felt a cool hand on my shoulder.

 170

"Lily," came Bonnie's soothing voice, "Paris is part of your Inner Universe now. You can visit anytime you want."

I can't say I fully bought Bonnie's claim. If that were true, and you only had to visit a place once and then could go back to your Inner Universe, I don't think the airline industry would be doing so well. Cruise ships, luxury resorts, they'd all go belly-up.

But I did get on the plane.

FROM THE PARISIAN DIARY OF
Lily M. Blennerhassett

Our journey has come to an end. As the plane bears us up into golden sunlight toward our fine home country, we are privileged with one final view of Paris, which now resembles nothing so much as a stately, elegant woman bejeweled and immaculately coiffed. Her gifts to us have been of art and architecture, of cuisine and culture, of sight and sound. She has changed us permanently; she has imprinted herself upon our souls. Perhaps this is what Hemingway meant when he said Paris was a movable feast, for a vestige of its riches and treats do indeed follow us home.

As for our little group, Janet is already hogging the closest bathroom, Charlotte and Lewis look suspiciously like two people about to become an item, Tim is getting quite used to speaking out loud in Actual Conversation, and Bonnie has picked up a regal medieval glow that I don't believe she had before visiting the Hôtel de Sens. I'm sure even Bud and Chaz have changed, though I think it may only have been from tossing an American sort of ball to tossing a European sort of ball.

On a personal note, I have to say I did not get what I originally thought I wanted out of Paris. My plan was to collect gems and nuggets to convert into the first chapter of my Great Parisian Novel. I was going to wander the realms Far Removed from the Regular People and the Simple Tourists. But the truth is, I was not transported into an elegant world of pâté de foie gras and champagne. The truth is, I don't have to write the Great Parisian Novel to be interesting. Sometimes the ordinary contains all the extraordinary a writer could ever need. My experience was what I swore it wouldn't be: that of a Simple Tourist. And you know what? This Simple Tourist had a blast.

Au revoir, Paris.
I have a feeling I'll be back.

LILY M. BLENNERHASSETT'S
CONCISE FRENCH GLOSSARY

eh bien: well, then

quatre, cinq, six: four, five, six

Bonjour! Comment ça va?: Hello! How are you?

vraiment fantastique: really fantastic

C'est formidable!: It's tremendous!

le chocolat: chocolate

commes les Françaises: As Frenchwomen do

la turbulence: turbulence

alors, mes enfants: now, my children

oui: yes

Allons-y: Let's go

chaussures: shoes

la grand-route: the highway

Ville Ecole Internationale: International School City

les bandits: robbers

les Français: the French

Ecoutez, mes enfants: Listen, my children

immédiatement: immediately

Pour les filles, deuxième étage: For the girls, second floor

Pour les garçons, troisième étage: For the boys, third floor

premier étage: first floor

rez-de-chaussée: street level

Voilà!: There it is!

allez: go

Bon appétit!: Hearty appetite!

steak au poivre: steak with peppercorns

escargots: snails

pommes de terre: potatoes

terrine: pâté

Voici!: Here it is!

raison d'être: reason for being

J'aime Nutella!: I love Nutella!

seul: alone

écrivain: writer

absolument: absolutely

D'accord?: Do you agree?

le bus: the bus

Comprenez?: You understand?

trop vite: too fast

la vie: life

rester: to rest

je veux: I want

s'il vous plaît: please

terrible: terrible

l'hôtel: hotel, manor, or other fancy building

une Parisienne: a Parisian woman

formidable!: tremendous, fabulous!

Bonjour! Je m'appelle Jah-nay!: Hello! My name is Jah-nay!

Je ne parle que français: I speak only French

la disgrâce: a disgrace

Pardon?: Excuse me?

Tu es perdu, ma petite poulette? Are you lost, my little chicken?

Mais tu parles un peu français, non?: But you speak a little French, no?

Chez: at the home of

Jean-Michel, nous avons besoin d'aller au Musée du Louvre tout de suite, s'il te plaît. La demoiselle ici est bien en retard.: Jean-Michel, we must go to the Louvre Museum right away, please. The young lady here is late.

Nous sommes arrivés: We have arrived

Magnifique, n'est-ce pas? Magnificent, right?

amusement: amusement

en bonne santé: in good health

objets: little thingies

fermé: closed

le chien de garde: the watchdog

Allô, oui? Je m'appelle Jahnay, et je suis une américaine qui a visité le Cimetière Père Lachaise. Maintenant mes deux amies sont accidentellement fermées dedans. . . . Oui? . . . Oui? Formidable, merci bien: Hello, yes? My name is Jah-nay, and I am an American who has visited the Père Lachaise Cemetery. Now my two friends are accidentally locked inside. . . . Yes? . . . Yes? Wonderful, thank you.

Merci bien, monsieur: Thank you very much, sir

Il n'y a pas de quoi, petite demoiselle. J'espère que ta voyage est bien agréable.: You're welcome, young lady. I hope you have a nice trip.

garçon-fille, garçon-fille: boy-girl, boy-girl

abats à l'etouffée: stewed organ meats

civelles: baby eels

cervelles de veau provençal: calf brains with garlic, tomatoes, and olive oil

agent de police: police officer

voyage: trip

représentants: representatives

sophistiqué: sophisticated

Où est la toilette?: Where is the bathroom?

au revoir: good-bye (literally, till we see each other again)

Bonjour. Je m'appelle Lily M. Blennerhassett, et je suis ravie de gagner le Prix Magnifique du Touriste Simple, qui honore l'auteur qui a écrit le livre le plus

réussi et brilliant du monde: Hello. I'm Lily M. Blennerhassett, and I'm thrilled to win the Magnificent Prize of the Simple Tourist, which honors the writer who has written the most Brilliant and Bestselling Book in the World.

ELIZABETH CODY KIMMEL

has visited Paris several times, and she has never been Separated from the Group. However, she was locked in a *cimetière* once after dark while guard dogs were on duty. Ms. Kimmel is the author of several *magnifique* books, including *Lily B. on the Brink of Cool* and *Lily B. on the Brink of Love*. She lives with her husband, daughter, and beagle in New York's Hudson Valley, far from the *sophistiqué* City of Lights. You can visit her online at www.codykimmel.com.